FOR SALE BY KILLER

CATHERINE BRUNS

FOR SALE BY KILLER
a Cindy York Mystery

by

CATHERINE BRUNS

Second Edition

Cover design by Yocla Designs

❀ Created with Vellum

ACKNOWLEDGMENTS

So many people played a pivotal role in the creation of this book, and I am truly grateful to each and every one of them. First, I must thank my main source of information, retired Troy police captain Terry Buchanan, who answers every one of my questions without complaint. Big hugs to my former manager and real estate expert, Mary Peyton, who never fails to fill in the blanks. Huge appreciation to Elena Hartwell for sharing her knowledge of tarot with me. Beta reader Constance Atwater always comes through whenever I need her. To my family and especially my very patient husband, Frank, for putting up with all those two o'clock in the morning plot questions. Last but not least, a heartfelt thank you to publisher Gemma Halliday and her team of editors for giving me the opportunity to breathe life into Cindy, her family and friends. It's been a fun ride.

CHAPTER ONE

The air was crisp and clean and smelled of freshly fallen snow that invaded my lungs as I breathed it in. Ah, much better. The drive would be good for me, and my sleep deprived brain sorely needed a wake-up call.

Winter had been long and dreary, and it was only the end of January. There were at least six more weeks until spring—not that I was counting. Days like this were normal in Upstate New York, but I had been tired of snow since Thanksgiving. My emotions were all over the place—I was irritable, moody, and restless. I tried to hide it from my husband, Greg, but wasn't always successful.

"Hang on, honey," he'd gently say to me. "Only a few more weeks left to go."

I shuffled my boots through the new inches of white stuff on the sidewalk, tempted to grab a shovel but knowing full well that Greg would bawl me out if I even so much as thought about cleaning snow in my present condition. Instead, I wrapped my wool coat closer around my cumbersome body and proceeded carefully toward my warm and cozy vehicle. The present of a car starter for Christmas had been a godsend.

With the kids in school, I needed to hit the pavement, so to speak. The question was, should I go to the office to answer phones in hopes of a new lead or drive around looking for houses for sale by owner?

A sharp kick from my stomach distracted me from my thoughts for a second. I smiled and placed my hands over my enormous belly. "Something tells me you are going to be quite a handful."

At the age of forty-four, this was to be my fourth child. The pregnancy hadn't been an easy one, and it had also been a total shock to both Greg and me, but we had gradually come to terms with it and were now looking forward to meeting our daughter soon.

I sighed and pushed the seat back further, since my stomach seemed to have grown again since yesterday. My cell rang from inside my purse, and after repositioning myself, I was able to dangle my hand down over the side of the console and grab it off the floor. At eight months pregnant, the car had finally run out of room for me. I placed the vehicle back in park and pressed the talk button on my phone. "Hey boss."

"How's little mama doing today?" the male voice on the other end asked. Jacques Forte was my dearest friend and the owner of Forte Realty, where I worked. He was another one of my blessings that I counted on a daily basis.

I laughed. "For the record, there's nothing little about me these days. Baby and I are going out for a drive to try to find some sales."

"I'll be at the office until pretty late tonight," Jacques said. "Stop by later if you get a chance."

Something in his tone was off. "Everything okay?"

"Just fine," he replied.

The weariness in his voice couldn't fool me though. "No new listings this week?" Jacques was a fantastic real estate broker and mentor to me. The winter had been especially horrible, and our area had been blanketed in at least a hundred inches of snow—so far. Most of New York State was in somewhat of a slump as far as home sales were concerned. Interest rates had risen, and many people were waiting until the spring to buy or put their houses on the market.

Still, I sensed that there was something else bothering Jacques. "So, everything is okay both business and personal wise?"

There was a moment's hesitation. "Look, love. You have enough to worry about without hearing my sob story."

"Hey," I said gently. "You're my best friend, and I only want to help. Is it Ed again?"

Jacques and Ed Kapinski had been married for almost two years. The manager of a local upscale restaurant, Ed was as devoted to his job as Jacques was to his real estate agency, meaning that both men were workaholics. Jacques didn't talk much about his personal life—even with me—but I knew they'd been having problems lately. Last week I had come into the office very early one morning after a sleepless night and found Jacques crashed on the couch in his office.

"We can talk about it later," Jacques said. "If you stop by the office, that is."

"I'll be there. First I want to drive around and see if I spot any FSBOs."

He coughed into the phone. "You need to be careful, darling. It just snowed, and the walkways are slippery. Let's face it, you aren't exactly your graceful self these days."

"I already know how big I am, thank you very much." Annoyance crept into my voice. "They've plowed the main road, and I've got my boots on. I'm only going for a drive, Mother. No ice skating, I promise."

He sighed. "Sarcasm becomes you, darling. *Not.* Oops, there's the office phone. See you soon."

I clicked off and placed the car in drive. It was probably best to take the highway and then travel further north into the Clifton Park and Saratoga areas. Besides being known for their popular horse racing season in the summer, Saratoga had some of the most refined and priciest homes in the state. I had looked on the Multiple Listing Service for expired listings this morning and found a handful in the area that had not been relisted yet. There was a chance they were now being offered as FSBOs—For Sale by Owners. Perhaps there was a seller out there waiting for a very pregnant real estate agent to descend upon them with an offer of representation they couldn't refuse.

Once the baby arrived it would be difficult for me to get out as often, so today seemed like a good time. Jacques had already assured me I could come back to work whenever I wanted and bring her with me. I had my own office to nurse her in private, but it would still take quite a bit of juggling.

I was so lost in my own thoughts that I drove right past the appropriately named Winter Road, where one of the expired listings was located. I realized my mistake too late and turned down the next street. My hopes to do a U-turn were dashed because of an oncoming car in the opposite direction and a truck following too closely behind me. I continued down the street called Rodgers Way and wondered if it somehow might connect to the next street.

As I continued down the road at a sedate twenty miles an hour, I noticed there were only a handful of houses on it. They were spread apart at quite a distance from each other, and the two mansions I noticed were older, perhaps from the nineteenth century.

The truck had turned off, and at the last second, I realized that Rodgers Way was a dead end. I pulled into the nearest driveway to turn my car around. Then I noticed a large home set back from the road at a considerable distance. The long, winding driveway had not been plowed and ended before a spectacular-looking Queen Anne Victorian mansion. I loved anything Victorian, and while the house was enough to give me pause, the generic-looking sign attached to the bottom of the mailbox nearly stopped my heart. Written in black felt-tip marker were four words that brought music to my ears: *For Sale by Owner*.

I put the car in all-wheel drive and started up the driveway's incline, my tires spinning slightly due to the snow that had accumulated. It was only a few inches, so I had little difficulty. While the long winding driveway helped to assure the mansion's privacy, it must have been a headache to clear in the winter, not to mention a small fortune. I stared in awe at the house, which was probably from the late nineteenth century. Carved stone ran around the bottom half of the mansion and veranda, with gray clapboard on the upper half that included two signature towers, one that I surmised was an attic.

Holy cow. Had I stumbled upon a hidden treasure or what?

As I grabbed my briefcase and wriggled myself out of the car, I took another look around. Upon closer inspection, the stone on the veranda was broken in several places and the clapboard needed a good pressure washing. For a brief second, I hesitated. Was there a chance the house would look better on the inside or worse? It was always a gamble. Oh, the heck with it. At this point, what did I have to lose?

I walked carefully up the steps to the veranda. The oak front door was chipped in several spots but had a lovely pane of Tiffany stained glass in the center. Despite the covered area, the veranda was slippery in a few spots. I rapped the brass knocker and waited. No answer. The owners were probably at work, so I took out one of my business cards and wedged it in the side of the door. They might call me. Then again, they might not. When I got home, I could check out the address on the MLS and see whom the house belonged to or even pop one of my flyers into the mail. At the present time, there was nothing else I could do.

As I lowered my right foot onto the top step, my left one slid forward. In a panic, I grabbed the rail with both hands, but my right foot slid out from underneath me, despite my rubber-soled boots. I landed with a thud on my backside at the edge of the veranda. Terrified for a moment, I continued to lay there. My first thought was for the baby's safety. I ran my hands over my stomach and, to my relief, felt a sharp kick. Still, I'd call my doctor to be on the safe side. I grabbed for the rail and struggled to raise myself when I felt a pair of hands on my shoulders. With a shriek, I tried to turn my head.

"Relax. Let me help you to your feet, ma'am." The man put his hands on my waist, and I stiffened, not sure who he might be. That was a pitfall of being a real estate agent. You never knew if a potential client might be lying in wait to harm you. Several of these horror stories had been featured on the news recently, and I had no desire to become the next victim.

Once I was standing on my own again, I stared up at the man, who was well over six feet tall. "Thank you. Are you the owner?"

"Yes, ma'am." He appeared to be in his sixties, with a shock of white hair and sallow-looking skin that made me wonder if he'd been ill recently. Despite the cold, he wore a short-sleeved black T-shirt, his lower arms covered by various tattoos.

"Percy Rodgers." He extended a hand for me to shake as his gaze fell upon my stomach. My coat had come unbuttoned during the fall, and my current condition was obvious to him as I watched his dark eyes widen in alarm. "Oh wow, I'm so sorry. Are you sure you're okay? I didn't realize you were expecting."

"That's all right, and yes, I'm fine. Cindy York with Forte Realty."

His eyes took on a hungry look at my words, and I nervously took an abrupt step backward. "Well, I should be going. You have my card."

Percy swallowed hard. "Hold on. You're a real estate agent? Gee, that's great. Would you like to come inside for a tour?"

This part of the job always gave me pause, and Percy's wolf-like eyes made me uneasy. After a few encounters with psychopathic killers in the past, I carried mace in my handbag. The incidents had left me guarded and feeling a tad vulnerable. "Uh, yes, I'd like that but need to answer this text from my office first."

He held the front door open for me. As I stepped into the foyer, I shot off a quick text to Jacques. *I'm at 25 Rodgers Way checking on a new listing. If you don't hear from me in thirty minutes, call to make sure I'm okay.* This was common practice for us, and Jacques was protective of all his employees but especially me these days. "Do you live here alone?"

Percy nodded as he took my coat and hung it inside the oak closet. "Yes. My grandmother left me the house in her will. She died last year, and I've been here for about three months now."

"I see." My first thought was why he would want to sell, but it seemed rude to ask outright. Money was the obvious reason, although I suspected it might be something else. The man did not look well. Percy's pallor was unhealthy, and his hands shook constantly. Maybe he was looking for a state with a warmer climate year-round.

"Would you like some coffee or tea, Mrs. York?" he asked.

"Please call me Cindy, and no thanks." I followed him into a spacious-sized great room. The mansion had hardwood floors throughout that were in desperate need of refinishing, but I could visualize how fabulous the place would look with them redone. A stone fireplace was on one side of the room, next to a window seat with colorful antique glass bottles displayed in a row. A large bay window looked out onto the front yard that was home to a row of evergreens, which nicely maintained the mansion's privacy from the road. High vaulted ceilings with large raised oak beams gave the open floor plan an even roomier feel. The formal dining room could be seen through the archway and another oak door that probably led to a kitchen. French doors on the other side of the great room looked out onto a backyard patio covered with at least a foot of snow.

Percy grinned sheepishly, having guessed my thoughts. "Yeah. I need to get someone out here to do some shoveling. Do you have a teenaged son who might be interested in the job? I'd pay him something for his time."

I laughed. "Well, I have a sixteen-year-old daughter but can assure you, that's one job she doesn't want. I'd be happy to ask around for you though."

Percy placed his hands on his narrow hips. "I do what I can but have emphysema. My doctor has strictly advised against any demanding physical labor. Can you believe I'm only 52? Most people think I'm 72."

My facial expressions were usually a dead giveaway, and hopefully that wasn't the case this time. "I'm sorry about your health." Percy's medical condition helped explain his sickly color.

Percy smiled and waved a hand dismissively. "Forget it. Let me show you around." He led the way to a kitchen filled with stainless-steel appliances. The floor was an expensive wood grain but also needed refinishing. While Percy filled a kettle from the sink, I noticed the large water stain in the ceiling above his head. This was a terrific house, but my brain was busy calculating the costs of potential repairs, and I didn't like the sum it was coming up with.

"There are five bedrooms and three bathrooms upstairs," he said. "Two of the bedrooms and one bathroom are on the third floor. The attic is on the fourth." He pointed to two separate doors that led off the kitchen. "There's a pantry through that door and a partial bath behind the other. All the bathrooms are done in marble. My grandmother loved the stone. I've been meaning to hire someone to refinish the floors but don't have enough money to spare right now and want to unload the house as soon as possible."

Older mansions always fascinated me. "I'm guessing from the looks of the home that it was built in the late 1800s?"

Percy placed the kettle on the gas stove. "You certainly know your houses, Cindy. My great-great-grandfather built this house for his bride in 1894. When they both died, the house was passed down to their son, and then it ended up with my grandmother." He sat down at the small table and gestured for me to join him. A tattoo on his wrist of a watch without hands caused a stirring of familiarity within me. There was some type of symbolism attached to it, but for the life of me I couldn't remember what.

"You do realize the house would fetch a much better price if the work was done, especially given today's market," I said. "What condition are the bedrooms in upstairs?"

Percy scratched his head thoughtfully. "Well, they need painting and the floors are a mess, but other than that the house is structurally sound. Very good bones." He looked at me, hope registering in his eyes. "I've been trying to advertise the place but don't have a clue as to what I'm doing. Would you be interested in taking the listing?"

My heart leapt at his words. If I could sell this house, it would be mean an enormous commission. I tried not to let the prospect of sudden cash cloud my brain and think about this in a rational manner instead. "Yes, I'd be interested. What do you have it advertised for?"

The kettle whistled, and Percy grabbed a mug from one of the white cabinets overhead with glass panes. "To be honest, I was hoping for about a million and a half. That's what I've told the few people who have called."

As quickly as my heart had leapt, it now sank to the bottom of my stomach. "I'm going to be honest with you, Percy. There's no way you're going to get that much money for this house in the condition it's in. I would suggest setting the asking price a few hundred grand lower."

He knit his brows together. "But shouldn't you price it higher because people are always going to offer lower anyway?"

"No." That was one of the first rules we'd learned in Real Estate 101. "That doesn't work. You should always price it as close as possible to what the real value is. Now, I haven't seen the entire house yet, and I'd have to run some comps first, but—"

Percy stirred his tea. "What are comps?"

"Comparables. Homes similar to yours that have sold in the area recently."

He looked disappointed. "I understand but really need to unload the house as soon as possible. Whatever you suggest is fine by me. What percentage of commission do you take?"

I must have heard him wrong. Owners always finagled over the starting price with me. "Generally, it's seven percent, but since this is what we deem to be a 'fine home,' I'll do it for six percent." A very healthy commission indeed for Forte Realty and me. Despite the crappy market, Jacques always had a prominent client or two who was looking for a mansion, and Saratoga was a very desirable area. It was still convenient but far enough away from the main roads to be considered country.

Percy drew a long breath. "Fine. Do you happen to have a listing agreement with you?"

For a moment I thought I must have been dreaming. Listings of this size didn't waltz into my life every day and not this easily. "Let me grab one from my briefcase." My fingers shook as I set it on the white Hillsdale kitchen table and drew out a standard contract. I stopped to fill in his name, address, and the amount we had agreed upon.

"There are some other forms I need for you to sign as well. The property disclosure and a few that are self-explanatory. For now, I can at least get the ball rolling tonight. I'll set up the listing online and call you with any questions I might have. Is the house listed on Zillow?" Zillow was a popular site for FSBO homes. If already there, it would be easier for me to copy a lot of the information from the site instead of asking Percy ten thousand questions.

"Yes, it is."

After we had both signed the forms and discussed other details, I jotted down a cell phone number for Percy then closed my briefcase with a click of satisfaction. As I grabbed my car keys out of my purse, I noticed that there was a voicemail displayed on my screen, probably from Jacques. Shoot. I had forgotten to take my phone off silent, and he might be worried about me. Without listening to the message, I dashed off a quick text. *Everything okay. See you at the office in about thirty minutes.* There was barely enough time to stop in and see him before heading home. My nine-year-old twins would be arriving from school in less than two hours.

"I'll have the sign man out here tomorrow or the day after at the latest." We walked toward the foyer together and I had a strong, sudden desire to skip gleefully.

"Are you sure you won't join me for a cup of tea before you leave?" he asked. "I'd enjoy the company."

"Thanks, but I need to get back to the office."

"Well, I'm very glad that you came by, Cindy. It gets pretty lonely out here, especially on dreary winter days like today." Percy gestured at my stomach. "How many children does this make for you?"

I grinned. "This is my fourth."

He seemed visibly impressed. "That's wonderful. You're very lucky. I always wanted children, but sadly, it didn't work out."

Percy was a nice man, and I felt sorry for him, but something about him waved a red flag of alarm. Maybe I was being overly cautious. "Don't you have any family?"

Percy shook his head with apparent regret. "A sister and

brother, but we don't talk much. My wife died many years ago." He stared out the colored front door pane as I studied his profile—the dark listless eyes, sunken cheeks, thin pale lips, and white whiskers surrounding them. "I need to get away from here. Even though I grew up in New York, I've never been fond of the state or its weather." He looked at the winter wonderland in his front yard. "I hate snow. It's so sterile, lifeless." His voice was hollow. "I don't belong here."

A chill settled between my shoulder blades, and for a moment, I wondered if I should go through with the listing since my gut seemed to be telling me not to. How foolish. I was only representing a client. There was no reason to get personally involved with him. The man wanted to sell his house, and I was providing the service. Why did I always have to be so suspicious of everyone?

"I promise to do everything I can to sell your house as soon as possible."

Percy flashed me a grateful smile. "Thank you for coming by, Cindy. Can I help you to your car?"

I shook my head. "I'm fine. It was nice to meet you, Percy. I'll call later when the house is up on the Multiple Listing Service."

I turned the car around in the driveway and glanced in my rearview mirror. Percy was still standing in the doorway, waving at me. I grinned to myself. Jacques was going to be thrilled when he found out. He needed the listing for the agency almost as much as I did. I pressed the hands-free on my steering wheel and instructed it to call Jacques. He answered on the second ring. "Hey, boss."

"Thank God," he murmured. "Are you still at that house on Rodgers Way?"

"No, I just left. Didn't you get my text? I said everything was fine."

Jacques let out an audible sigh of relief. "For a moment I was worried that maybe you had gone ahead and signed a contract to list the place."

My blood turned to ice at the words. Had my premonition been right? "Actually, I did sign a contract with the owner. His name is Percy Rodgers."

There was dead silence on the other end for at least ten seconds. "Please tell me that you're joking," Jacques finally said in a hoarse voice.

"Okay, you're really scaring me now." I slid the car to a stop before a red light that had changed at the last second. "Tell me what's going on. What's wrong with that house?"

"There's nothing wrong with the house," Jacques said. "Apparently you never read the newspaper, my dear."

Impatient, I bit into my lower lip. "For God's sake, tell me what's going on."

"Percy Rodgers got out of jail a few months ago," Jacques said. "After he served twenty years for killing his wife. You just agreed to represent a killer, Cin."

CHAPTER TWO

"Okay." Jacques leaned forward over the mahogany desk, his sharp green cat-like eyes peering out at me from underneath Prada bifocals. "Let's not fly off the handle here. We'll simply talk about this in a calm and rational manner."

I struggled not to roll my eyes. Jacques was good-natured, excellent at his job, a great boss, and a devoted friend. We had met about five years ago when we'd both been employed by Hospitable Homes, my first job as a licensed real estate agent. The manager had hated me and done everything in her power to make my life miserable. To make matters worse, a co-worker who had been stealing my listings was later murdered and I found myself at the top of the suspect list. Had it not been for Jacques, I might not have survived in the business for very long.

Jacques' office, like him, was stylish and modern. Expensive silver-framed artwork lined the white walls, and a built-in mahogany bookcase ran along one side, filled with every type of real estate literature one could possibly imagine. An exercise bike dominated the other side, and in between was a pristine white leather couch with matching armchairs on each side, strategically placed in front of a gas fireplace.

I sat in one of the padded chairs stationed in front of his desk. These were generally used for clients or, in my situation, an employee who might need a bit of a tongue lashing.

"Is this why Percy had the house for sale by owner?" I asked. "Because no one would represent him?"

Jacques smoothed his striped blue and white silk tie that went well with his immaculately pressed navy suit. "The guy has had it on the market ever since he got out of prison. Guess Mr. Rodgers needs a new neighborhood to play in." He ran a hand through his thick mass of blond hair. "Seriously, Cin, how could you *not* have known?"

My face grew warm. "Sorry. I've been a little too busy to read the paper lately. Besides, he doesn't have to disclose jail to potential buyers."

"No, but most people in the area already know. Didn't you think it was odd that no one else had offered to sell it for the guy?" Jacques asked. "Sure, the place needs work, but it's one of those historical homes that people always fall in love with. Wasn't there anything that warned you?"

"Well, I do remember that he had a weird tattoo on his wrist. A watch without hands. I've seen that somewhere before—"

Jacques pressed his lips together tightly. "You're not very versed in prison lingo, are you?"

"And you are, Mr. Ralph Lauren?" I scoffed.

He ignored my remark. "A watch without hands signifies a long sentence in jail. Didn't you think it was strange that he accepted the first agent who happened to drop by? Especially when almost every agent in this state is hungry for a deal given the dismal market?"

Jacques was doing a great job at getting under my skin. "No, not really. Maybe I thought things were finally starting to go my way."

Jacques face softened. "I'm sorry, darling. No one deserves a fat paycheck more than you. But I'd rather not see you get sliced up like his former wife."

Yikes. "I don't know the whole story." Actually, I knew nothing of Percy Rodgers' personal history. "What exactly happened?"

Jacques laced his fingers together and placed them behind his head as he leaned back in the chair. "It's quite simple, really. He suspected his wife was fooling around on him. You know the deal. She was beautiful and young but penniless, while his family had money. They were only married a few years before Percy began to get suspicious that there was someone else and even hired a private detective to follow her around."

I leaned forward in my chair—well, as much as it was possible. "Go on."

"One day, Vanessa Rodgers was supposed to go shopping with her sister-in-law. The woman showed up at Vanessa and Percy's house and found Vanessa bleeding to death on the kitchen floor. Percy was supposedly out on an errand but had no alibi. The private investigator even swore under oath in court that Percy had called his wife a lying, cheating bitch. Plus, his fingerprints were all over the murder weapon. The jury found Percy guilty and sentenced him to twenty-five years to life. He was released early on good behavior. It was all over the papers when he got out of prison."

"Well, obviously his grandmother didn't believe he killed his wife," I retorted. "She left her house to him."

Jacques fiddled with a crystal paperweight on his desk. "From what I've heard, his grandmother, Stella Rodgers, was quite eccentric and suffered from dementia. She was first diagnosed shortly after he went to prison and grew gradually worse over the years. I don't know when her will was made, but maybe she was forced to leave the mansion to him."

"What are you saying? That Percy held a gun to his grandmother's head and demanded she give him the house?"

Jacques narrowed his eyes. "Don't joke about this stuff. I did a little checking with an estate attorney I know while you were on your way back here. He's familiar with the Rodgers' situation, although he couldn't tell me much. It seems that the grandmother's will has not gone through probate yet. In most instances this means there are probably some relatives still contesting a portion of it."

I shifted in my seat. The baby was kicking up a storm, and my lower back was killing me as a result. "Does that mean that he's not allowed to list it? My contract could be voided without an issue, right?"

Jacques shook his head. "No, it's his to do with as he pleases." His eyes were full of sympathy. "Cin, this is your listing, and you can certainly do as you please, but you're also one of my employees, not to mention my dearest friend. Frankly, I'm concerned for your welfare. What if the house doesn't sell and he decides to take his anger out on you?"

I laughed out loud. "Come on. Don't you think that's a bit extreme?"

He looked at me soberly. "We can't be too careful these days. A fellow real estate agent that I knew relocated three years ago and ran a very successful agency in Kansas. Last year, she showed a house to a man she'd never met before. Lily didn't come home. They found her dead body a couple of days later, buried behind the house she'd showed him." He lowered his eyes to the desk and played with the paperweight again, but I could see the color rising in his cheeks. "She was also pregnant."

The baby kicked again, as if giving her vote in the decision. Jacques' story chilled me, and I rubbed my arms in hopes of sudden warmth. This wasn't only about me. I had a life inside me, and she had to come first. While Greg knew nothing of the listing yet, I had a strong suspicion he'd feel the same way as Jacques. "Why didn't you tell me about Lily before?"

Jacques' eyes started to cloud over. "I think you know why."

Oh boy. I swallowed a huge gulp of air. "Maybe you're right."

"Why do you think I'm licensed to carry?" Jacques asked. "Because it's not safe out there for real estate agents these days. Any whack job can ask you to show him a house."

Jacques kept his gun under the front seat of his convertible, a practice I never quite understood. If he didn't know the people he was meeting, he'd usually bring it inside the house with him. Jacques preferred not to keep the weapon in his own house since Ed was not a fan of guns. These days they didn't need another bone of contention between them.

"All right, I agree this isn't a good time for me to be taking any unnecessary risks. I've never tried to get out of a listing agreement before, though." Heck, it was all I could do to find them, let alone get rid of one. "Is the process difficult?"

Jacques rose from his chair and came around to the other side of the desk. "Not at all. We'll get him to sign an unconditional release so that both of you are relieved from the contract without further involvement. Do you need the form?"

"No, I'm sure I have the file and can print one out when I get home. I'd better get going. The twins will be home in a little while." I heaved myself out of the seat. "It just goes to show that whenever something sounds too good to be true, it probably is."

Jacques' expression was grim. "I know things look kind of bleak now, and we sure as hell could have used that listing. But I'd never forgive myself if something happened to you, Cin. You realize that this has nothing to do with my faith in your abilities, right? I wouldn't want any of my agents to take the house. It's a hell of a scary world out there, and safety always comes first."

I bent down to grab my briefcase off the floor, but Jacques

was quick to get there first. "Let me get it before you topple over, darling."

"Funny," I mocked as he handed it to me. "All right. I'll call Percy when I get home."

Jacques raised his eyebrows. "Do you want me to do it? I'll be here pretty late."

"No, it's my listing, so I should be the one to take care of it." I glanced over at the sofa. There was a blanket folded over one arm. "You're not staying here again tonight, are you?"

His face grew crimson. "The office is comfortable, and if it snows like they said it would, I might since—"

"Jacques," I cut him off. "What is going on? Have you and Ed officially separated?"

Jacques took his glasses off and polished them with a handkerchief. "We've been having some issues. As you know, I've wanted to adopt a child since we got married, but Ed feels he isn't ready for parenthood, especially a baby. I went ahead and did some checking around without his knowing because I thought he'd come to gradually accept the idea. The agency called a few weeks back with great news. There was a little girl available, only six months old. When I told Ed about it, he freaked, and we had a huge fight. I had no choice but to tell the agency no. God knows when we might get another chance. Since then, we've barely managed to tolerate one another."

My heart broke for him. I knew how much Jacques loved kids, and he was wonderful with Darcy, my sometimes snotty sixteen-year-old, and my exuberant nine-year-old twins, Stevie and Seth. I gently laid a hand on his arm. "When did all of this start?"

"Christmas," he said gruffly. "Great timing huh?"

My shoulders sagged. "Next time something like this happens, would you please let me know? Don't keep it all inside. That isn't good for you." I hesitated before asking my next question. "What does this mean for your marriage?"

"Don't ask me. I suggested counseling, and Ed went nuts. We've barely spoken in the last few weeks. The stress is so mind-blowing at times that I have to come here to get any work done and try to keep my sanity." Jacques' bright green eyes were dull as he stared at me.

"Could I talk to him?" I asked hopefully.

Jacques gave me a wan smile. "He didn't even want me to tell you about it, Cin. You know how private he is about everything. We'll have to see what happens. Maybe he'll come around eventually."

"I hate to see you hurting like this." Besides saving my life twice, Jacques had been such a generous and good friend. He always put everyone else first. "Why don't you come over to the house for dinner tonight?"

He shook his head. "Thanks, but I need to finish up a few things here. Call me after you've talked to Percy. If you plan to go back to his house tomorrow to give him a copy of the release, I want to go with you."

"It's not necessary."

"It is to me." He narrowed his eyes. "I know I don't say it enough, but I'm grateful for your friendship, Cin. Maybe I have a funny way of showing it."

"No worries. I know how difficult it is for you to open up sometimes. I'm just grateful to be a part of your life."

"WHAT'S FOR DINNER?" Stevie asked as both boys raced through the kitchen door, dropping books and snow everywhere. The school bus tooted its horn from outside, probably in apparent relief to be rid of them.

I turned around from the stove, where I was preparing chicken potpie and mashed potatoes, one of Greg's favorite meals. "Chicken pot pie."

"Why do they call it pot pie?" Stevie wanted to know as he grabbed a box of cookies out of the snack cabinet. "Do you make it in a pot?"

"No," I laughed. "It's cooked in the oven in a pie dish."

Both boys resembled their father, with their curly, light brown hair and blue eyes. Stevie was a carbon copy of Greg right now as a line deepened in his forehead, still trying to figure out the whole potpie scenario.

Seth said nothing as he slammed his books down on the kitchen table and then raced into the living room. Two seconds later I heard the television blaring.

"Hey," I called out. "No TV until your homework is done."

"Aw, Mom," he protested. "But SpongeBob is on."

I poked my head in the doorway. "SpongeBob is *always* on. You can watch it later."

He grumbled but shut the television off and came back out into the kitchen. Stevie had already settled into a chair with his science book open.

"Mom?" Stevie asked as I set a glass of milk in front of him. "When is the baby coming?"

"In about four weeks." I sat down at the table to peel potatoes. My lower back was hurting more than usual and made standing for long periods difficult. Then again, sitting wasn't much better.

"Grandma told someone on the phone the other night that you looked ready to pop," Stevie announced.

"Then she said you must have gained about fifty pounds," Seth put in.

I winced inwardly. "Grandma" referred to Helen York, Greg's mother. She had babysat the other night when Greg and I had gone out in search of a new stroller for the baby. She was sarcastic, humorless, and her mouth knew no filter. Helen had never been a fan of mine and even had the audacity to wear black to our wedding. Since she was the kids' only surviving grandparent, I tried to make the best of it. Lately I had been returning her snide remarks with a few of my own, which seemed to surprise her. Still, I didn't want to make an enemy of the woman. My own mother had died before the kids were born, and it would have been nice if Helen could have been a substitute one of sorts, or at least civil to me.

After the twins had finished their homework and gone downstairs to the family room, I went into the study and shut the door behind me. Patrick Star's laughter resonated from the floor underneath me while I logged into my laptop. I hated to make this call and, despite everything, somehow still felt sorry for Percy. Maybe I wasn't the greatest judge of character, but he didn't strike me as a killer. Then again, I'd met several during my lifetime, and they hadn't exactly been wearing signs either.

I googled Percy Rodgers' grandmother, Stella Rodgers. Her father had founded a mining company in Canada, and his entire estate had passed on to his only child when he and his wife had died. From the information I gathered, it appeared that Stella had never worked for a living and still owned several racehorses at the local track. She'd led a charmed life filled with boarding school, debutante balls, and a Cinderella-type affair wedding.

There was no sense in putting it off any longer. I closed out Google and dialed the number Percy had given me. It was picked up on the third ring. "Hello."

"Hi, Percy. It's Cindy York from Forte Realty."

"Oh, hi, Cindy. Don't tell me you've found a client already. Gee, you work fast." He sounded out of breath. "I've been doing some last-minute cleaning around the house and don't think it will be ready to show until tomorrow. Later in the day would be better because I have someone stopping by."

This was going to be tougher than I thought. "That's not why I called. I'm afraid that I can no longer represent you."

There was an ominous silence on the other end of the line. "I see," Percy finally said. "May I ask why?"

My stomach muscles tightened, probably a combination of a false contraction and the uncomfortableness of the situation. "I don't think I'm the right agent for the job."

Another silence. God, talk about your awkward moments.

Percy breathed heavily into the phone, and then to my amazement, he burst into laughter. "God, Cindy. Why don't you tell me the truth?"

"I don't know what you mean," I lied.

"Yes, you do. You found out I served time for killing my wife. Well, let me reassure you that I didn't kill her. Someone set me up."

I didn't want to have this conversation. "Look Percy, for what it's worth, I believe you. The fact is that I'm eight months pregnant and not sure that I can deal with any additional stress right now."

"Well, you seemed more than willing to take it on before," he mocked. "Something has changed since earlier today. Why don't you come right out and admit you don't want to represent a killer? Or maybe you're convinced I'd kill a pregnant woman, just for kicks?"

Horrified, I placed a protective hand on my stomach. "I'll drop off an unconditional release form for you to sign tomorrow. If you'd rather not see me, it can be left in the mailbox. Once again, I'm sorry."

"Cindy, wait. Please!"

My finger hovered over the disconnect button, but I hesitated when I heard his plea. "Percy, I have to go."

"I didn't kill Vanessa, but I'm pretty sure I know who did. If you give me a few more days to prove it, then—"

My hand shook. "I hope this works out for you, but I need to think of my baby first." Even if I believed him, selling his house would still be stressful under the circumstances. True, people listing their homes for sale did not have to divulge prison time in New York State, but as Jacques said, almost everyone else in the area had already known about Percy—well, except for me. Having to hear the constant gossip plus Jacques breathing down my neck and Greg calling twenty times a day was bound to set me on edge. "Perhaps after I have the baby, if you haven't already found another agent, we can talk again."

Percy laughed—this time a cold, bitter one that blew through me like a sharp gust of wind. "Yeah, right. Do you think you were the first? Please don't flatter yourself. I've already contacted at least a dozen other agents. No one wants to represent me."

"Please, I—"

"Good luck with your baby. No hard feelings. As far as talking again, sure, no problem. If I'm still around, that is."

Percy's words unnerved me. "What do you mean? Where are you going?"

His only response was a sharp click as the line went dead.

CHAPTER THREE

"Look at this article on making borders for the baby's room." I pointed to a page in *Parents* magazine. Although not very crafty, I should be able to handle something that simple with all the instructions included.

Greg shut our bedroom door and locked it. The twins were already asleep, and Darcy was in her room doing homework. I'd heard her lilting voice a little while ago and suspected she was having a late-night gossip session with a girlfriend over boys, but I didn't have the energy to go down the hall and stop her.

A scratching noise sounded from the other side of the door. Greg opened it, and our cat, Sweetie, rushed in. She immediately jumped onto the bed and settled herself at the bottom.

Greg sighed and scratched his head. "Well, we have a few months before you have to worry about the border, sweetheart."

"I know, but after she gets here, I won't have as much time to think about it." The baby's room would in fact be *our* room for at least the next three months. Our house only had three bedrooms—Greg's and mine, the twins', and Darcy's. We could convert the study downstairs if necessary, but I liked the idea of having the baby close, especially since I would be nursing her every couple of hours to start. Greg planned to add on a room in the spring. We'd already looked into a home equity loan and been approved.

Although fifty and AARP loomed for Greg in a couple of years, he seemed to get better looking with age. He was lean and muscular, even though he didn't get much of a chance to work out at the gym these days. His curly light brown hair showed no signs of receding, his jaw was strong and defined, and those crystal blue eyes of his still made me swoon. They regarded me with love and warmth as he crossed the room and got into bed beside me.

"You did the right thing about that Rodgers guy, sweetheart. I would have been worried sick about you every minute of the day."

I cocked an eyebrow at him. "Okay, be honest. Would you have told me not to do it?"

He placed his arms around me, drawing me close. "Of course not. I trust your judgment. But I'd be lying if I said it didn't scare me." He ran a gentle hand over my stomach. "Your safety and hers always comes first."

"I can't believe she's almost here." We both looked over at the beechwood crib in the corner of the room that Greg had put together last month. I'd bought a beautiful pink and white crib set online that consisted of a bumper, comforter, fitted sheet, and matching diaper stacker. It was all set up and waiting for her. A *Sesame Street* mobile that a friend had given us dangled above the crib.

Greg kissed me tenderly on the lips. "Me neither, and that's another thing. This has been such a difficult pregnancy for you that the extra stress and worry about that house would not be doing you any favors right now."

"Maybe," I sighed, "but I am worried about money, or the fact that we never seem to have any. The real estate market had been so pitiful this winter that Jacques is going crazy."

"It'll get better. You let me worry about the money factor, baby." His voice was low and sexy and smooth, and when he kissed me again, desire stirred through me. The baby kicked underneath Greg's hand, and he laughed. "Guess she's telling me to knock it off."

I ran a hand down his smooth bare chest. "That's another reason I can't wait until she gets here."

He kissed me again and yawned, his hand still protectively on my stomach. "This baby still doesn't have a name. We need to agree on something soon."

"I know." After turning the lamp off on the nightstand, I tried to arrange myself in a comfortable position on my side. I used to love sleeping on my stomach, but those days were long gone. Greg draped an arm around me from behind, and I pressed my body into his. "How about Eileen, after my mother?"

His voice sounded sleepy in the darkness. "I took a girl named Eileen to the prom. She ended up ditching me for another guy. What about Helen?"

I winced. "After your mother?"

Greg chuckled. "I can see you're excited about that prospect. You might as well know that she did hint around about it, but I was noncommittal."

"Sorry, but no." It would have to be a cold day in hell first—or rather, colder than New York in January.

"How about for a middle name, then?"

His tone was warm and hopeful, and I hated to douse water on it. "I'd rather we used Eileen for her middle name. How about something that goes well with Darcy—Danielle, Dorothy, Denise?"

"Nah, I don't care for any of those."

I sighed. This had been a losing battle for the last few months. "At this rate, she won't have a name until she goes to kindergarten." I reached for his hand in the darkness. "I'm scared."

He snuggled closer and kissed me on the cheek. "Why, sweetheart? About the delivery?"

"No, not that. But I don't have as much energy as I did with the twins. I'm forty-four and need to be a good mother to this child. I want to be able to do all the things that I do for the boys."

"You will." He reached over me to snap the lamp back on and looked down at me, his crystal blue eyes filled with love. "It doesn't matter how old you are. You'll always be a wonderful mother. These kids are so lucky to have you." His voice turned gruff. "And me too."

He kissed me again, a long passionate one that made me want him even more. "Okay, you need to stop doing that." I laughed.

Greg's face was solemn as he continued to stare down at me. "Remember when you had complications a few months back and I had to rush you to the hospital?"

I closed my eyes in attempt to shut out the memory. That had been a terrible day. "I thought I was losing the baby."

Greg stroked my hair tenderly. "When we first found out about the pregnancy, I'll admit it was quite a shock to my system. I'd never even thought about another baby. It took a little while to get used to the idea, and I was preoccupied with how our lives were going to change. But that day when you had to go to the hospital, I was so afraid you might lose her." His voice broke, and my eyes watered in response. "That was when I suddenly couldn't comprehend her not being a part of our lives. I want this, Cin. I want her. This is meant to be, and there's no doubt in my mind that we'll be even happier than we were before."

A tear rolled down my cheek, and he gently swiped it away with his thumb. Greg had been so supportive during the entire pregnancy—through all of them, actually. To know that he'd had doubts too was surprising yet comforting. He always put the kids and me first. "I love you so much."

"I love you too." He kissed me again. "So you see, that's why I'm not concerned about this house or your client's hurt feelings. We have more important things to worry about. Jacques is going with you tomorrow, right?"

"Yes. He insisted."

"Good. I wouldn't want you to go confront that whack job yourself. And I don't want this guy making you upset, especially in your condition. Killers don't care about anyone else, sweetheart. You of all people should know that by now."

Boy, did I ever.

"You don't owe this guy anything," Greg continued. "So please stop feeling guilty."

"But I can't seem to forget what he said about being innocent on the phone earlier. It's been bothering me all night."

"You've got too big of a heart," he said and snuggled down beside me again. "Some of these characters can be awful shady. Didn't anyone ever tell you that real estate agents have to be cutthroat?"

With a shudder, I clicked off the light again. Within a minute Greg started to snore softly while I lay awake, staring into the darkness and thinking about his statement.

Greg didn't know this, but that had been a bad choice of words on his part. When I had googled Percy's name earlier this evening, I discovered that was how his wife had died. Someone had slit Vanessa Rodger's throat.

~

"THERE'S NOTHING TO be nervous about, darling." Jacques reached over to pat my arm as he maneuvered the steering wheel with his left hand.

"I'm not nervous," I said. "You really didn't need to bring me. I was perfectly capable of coming alone."

"Forget it," he growled. "I'm not taking any chances. This guy is a psycho."

Percy hadn't seemed crazy to me, but it was useless to argue. "There's a chance he might not even be home." I sounded a bit too hopeful. "Maybe I can leave the agreement in the mailbox, and he can email it back to me."

"Don't count on it, love. You know these things never work out the way we want them to."

He had a point. I thought about what I would say to Percy, but nothing sounded adequate enough. Frustrated, I watched Jacques as he drove.

"What?" he asked suddenly.

"Did you stay at the office again last night?"

Jacques pursed his lips together and didn't answer.

"Come on," I pleaded.

He shook his head stubbornly. "I don't want to get into this right now."

"Can I help it if I'm worried about you?"

Jacques took a left onto Rodgers Way and then cast a sideways glance at me. "I appreciate the thought, but you have enough going on in your own life to keep you preoccupied without worrying about mine."

"Will you please come to dinner tonight? The kids would love to see you, and I don't want you ordering takeout again at the office."

Jacques raised an eyebrow as he parked the car in Percy's driveway. "How did you know?"

"I saw the container in the garbage this morning. You can't avoid Ed forever. Go home tonight and talk to him."

"We'll see." He pushed his glasses closer to his eyes and stared out the window, mesmerized. "Wow. This is truly a shame. I love old Victorians like this, especially with verandas. Do you want me to come inside with you?"

I opened my door and looked down at the ground. To my relief, the driveway had been cleared. "No thanks. I'll be fine."

"I'll keep an ear out for you. Good luck, darling. Remember, if I don't see you in five minutes, I'm coming in."

Jeez Louise. "Don't you think that's a bit much?"

Jacques pulled his iPhone out of his pocket and started to scroll through his contacts. "No, I don't. Listen, I've got to check on a closing. Just give Mr. Rodgers his release papers and get the heck out of his neighborhood, okay? I'll see you in a few."

I was tempted to say something snarky but decided to keep my mouth shut. Jacques meant well and was only looking out for my welfare, but sometimes he was bit too overprotective, like a big brother or an overbearing father, so to speak.

Grumbling, I eased my body out of the seat, grateful for the flat, unattractive rubber boots I'd worn. I'd stopped worrying about making a fashion statement long ago.

Jacques rolled his window down. "Need some help, love?"

"No, I'll be fine." Fearful of taking another tumble, I walked slowly up the stairs of the veranda. My lower back was screaming in pain, and I suspected it might have something to do with the fall I'd taken yesterday. The baby seemed to have dropped a bit as well. I'd called my doctor this morning, but he was on vacation, and his nurse had assured me not to worry about the fall. I had an appointment to see him next week, and she said everything should be fine until then. Based on my history, they thought there was a good chance the baby might come a week or so early, and that sounded great to me.

I thumped the brass knocker against the door and waited. There was no answer, so after a minute I knocked again. Still no answer. Well, this was what I'd wanted, right? On a hunch, I decided to try the doorknob. To my surprise, it turned easily in my hands.

"Percy?" I entered the foyer and glanced around, but the house was as quiet as a tomb. Why had he left the door unlocked? He'd said something about expecting a visitor when we'd talked on the phone. I walked into the great room but saw no one around. Fear swept over me as a low moan sounded from behind the desk, causing me to jump.

Cautiously, I approached the long oak desk. The chair was lying on the floor next to it, and a sneakered foot was sticking out from behind the desk. I shrieked and got down on my knees as fast as was possible for me.

Percy was lying behind the desk. Blood had stained the entire front of his white Yankees T-shirt and spread to the wooden surface beneath him. His breathing was irregular and his face the color of a bedsheet. He opened one eye and stared at me in a confused haze. The fingers of Percy's right hand were curled around a sharp kitchen knife, also dripping with blood.

"Oh my God!" I screamed. "What happened?"

He reached his left hand out to me, and I gave a small audible whimper as his blood-soaked fingers connected with mine. "Dying." His speech was faint and somewhat garbled. I leaned closer in an attempt to hear him better. "Knew it would happen. Killed me the same—same way as Vanessa."

Bile rose in the back of my throat. Percy wasn't making any sense, but he needed help immediately or else he would wind up like his wife. I reached into my coat pocket for my phone. It wasn't there. I must have left it in the car. In desperation I tried to stand, but the baby gave a sudden kick so forceful that it hurt, sending me back down to my knees. "Percy, I'm going to get you help. Don't move. Try to stay calm, okay?"

He opened his mouth to say something, but no sound came out. I tried to get to my feet again but stumbled, whether from the pressure of the baby or sheer panic I wasn't sure. Like a helpless baby myself, I started to crawl toward the front door on all fours. "Jacques!" I screamed at the top of my lungs, praying that the window in his car was still down. "Jacques!"

Footsteps could be heard running up the veranda, growing louder by the second. Jacques rushed into the room and knelt beside me on the floor. "Oh my God, darling! Are you in labor?"

"No, I'm having trouble walking." It sounded sarcastic and almost comical but happened to be the truth. "Percy's bleeding. I don't know what happened to him, but it's not good. Call 9-1-1!"

Jacques immediately whipped out his phone as I crawled back over to Percy. The pressure in my bladder had become extremely painful, and I did my best to ignore it. Good grief. Leave it to me to need a bathroom at this moment. I touched Percy's hand again and tried to keep my voice steady, but it was impossible. "Percy? Hang on. Help is on the way. Don't leave us, okay?"

He opened his eyes again and stared at me. "I—didn't—"

"You didn't what?" Then I noticed the gash on his neck and drew back in horror. Dear God. Had someone stabbed him, or had Percy tried to kill himself? My thoughts drifted back to the article I'd read about his wife's murder so many years ago. Vanessa Rodgers had died in the same manner. Was this a coincidence? I didn't think so.

"Vanessa. Loved her. I—I couldn't hurt her, not ever. Her killer—here. Had to shut me...up. Find them—please."

He closed his eyes, and I waited, almost impatiently, for him to continue. "Find who? Percy, who did this to you?"

Percy wheezed out one long, faint breath and then lay still. I felt his limp wrist for a pulse, but there was no movement. I let go of his hand in fright and clamped a hand over my mouth. "Oh God."

"Thank you." Jacques spoke into the phone. "An ambulance will be here in a couple of minutes." He stood beside me, looking down at Percy, and his tanned complexion went gray. "Oh, dear Lord. It looks like we're too late."

I turned away from the body and started to pant, feeling completely out of sorts and unable to catch my breath. "He—he tried to tell me who did this. Percy—he couldn't get the words out."

Concern creased Jacques' face. He reached down and helped me to my feet. "You look awful, love. Are you okay?"

I placed a hand over my rock-hard belly. "I—need the bathroom. You called for an ambulance?"

Jacques nodded. "Yes. Do you need help finding one?" His phone buzzed. "Crap. This might be the police calling back. Hang on a second, love."

He walked away, and I took a step forward then stared down at the floor or, more specifically, at the puddle next to me. "Uh, wait. Yeah, I think I'm going to need some help."

"To the bathroom?" Jacques turned around and peered at me in concern from behind his glasses. Then his gaze shifted down to the floor. He uttered a guttural sound low in his throat. "Oh my Lord. Did you have an accident?"

He spoke to me almost reproachfully, as if I was a two-year-old. Despite everything that had happened, I fought a sudden comical urge to laugh and cry at the same time. "No. I think I just went into labor."

CHAPTER FOUR

After the EMT vehicle and police cars had arrived at the scene, Jacques rushed back to his car, where I was writhing in discomfort, cell phone in my hand. He was breathing so hard that he might have been in labor too.

"The cops have agreed to take my statement down at the hospital," he panted. "The next ambulance should be here any minute for you."

When another contraction came along, I groaned and sucked in a deep breath. "I can't get Greg on his phone. It keeps going to voicemail. Forget the ambulance. I don't want to ride in that thing. Can't you take me?"

"Well, yes." Jacques stared at me uneasily. "You won't have it on the way, right?"

"My hospital is only about fifteen minutes away. I think we'll be okay."

Jacques hesitated. "I hate to sound insensitive, darling, but please tell me you won't have another accident—this time on my leather seats."

I gave him my best murderous glare. "Never fear. Your water only breaks once."

Despite the cold temperature outside, Jacques mopped at his forehead with a handkerchief. "Well, that's a relief. Okay, I'll run back in and tell them that I'm taking you over. Stay put, love. Don't move."

Where does he expect me to go? I gripped the door handle tightly as another contraction swept over me and reminded myself that Jacques had probably never dealt with a woman in labor before. Dear God, I hoped this would be over soon. Labor for Darcy had been a brutal 36 hours. The twins had come early, about five weeks before their due date, and I'd needed an emergency C-section. My doctor had mentioned that we could try for a natural birth this time but there were no guarantees. That probably was not about to happen now.

Jacques ran back to the car and got behind the wheel. He tore out of the driveway like a crazy man. It had started to snow, and the road was covered. *Great. What else can go wrong?* I tried Greg's phone again then remembered he was going to lunch with some potential clients today and said he might be out of reach for a little while. He'd given me the name of the restaurant, but for the life of me, I couldn't remember it.

"No luck with hubby?" Jacques switched lanes illegally around another car that dared to go the speed limit, his tires sliding along the paved road.

"Slow down," I gasped. "We have plenty of time." At least I hoped so. Another contraction started, and I gritted my teeth against the pain. "Oh God. When was my last contraction?"

He turned to stare at me and almost veered into the other lane. "Am I supposed to be timing them?"

"Look out!" I screamed as he barely missed sideswiping a car.

"Sorry, love, but I'm a newbie at this." Sweat trickled down the side of Jacques' face. "That's one of the wonderful things about adoption. I wouldn't have to do that Lamaze stuff and remind you to breathe. Hey, what about the terrible twins? Aren't they due home soon?"

"Oh God." Sweat was forming a river on my forehead as well, and I had a sudden, strong urge to push. "I—I can't—Gotta call Darcy's cell." But I was too immobilized by the pain to do anything else but pant. "Can't you turn the heat down?"

"But the window will fog up, and I won't be able to see," Jacques protested. "You want to get there in one piece, don't you?"

"Right now, my goal is to get there," I croaked out.

"You sound like you stepped out of *The Exorcist*, love." He reached over to pat my hand. "I'll call Darcy and Greg. In the meantime, keep doing what you're doing."

"What does that even mean?" I looked up in time to see him run a red light. "Stop driving like a maniac. You're not helping!"

Jacques ignored my protest as he pulled into the emergency parking lot of the hospital. He left the vehicle at the curb and opened his car door. "Do you want a wheelchair?"

I held my stomach between my hands and started to pant. "Yeah. I don't think I can walk."

"I'm so glad I'm not a woman," Jacques muttered as he turned and ran toward the front entrance. He stumbled on the slick pavement and fell flat on his face. Dear God. What was happening to us? We were both a hot mess. Jacques never stumbled—in business or his personal life. He had gone from self-assured real estate broker to possible ditzy delivery room coach in a matter of minutes. I prayed that Greg would get my message soon, or with luck maybe he'd come right to the hospital. If only I could remember the name of the restaurant, but my mind kept drawing a blank.

As I sat there in discomfort, I tried to focus my attention on something else, but the only thing that kept coming to mind was Percy. The visual of his dead body gave way to another contraction. It was probably a safe assumption that finding him clinging to life had led to me going into early labor. His final words repeated themselves over and over in my head. "Find killer." This man, who I hadn't even known existed before yesterday, and the image of his brutal death would now stay with me forever.

Jacques came hurrying down the walkway with a nurse beside him pushing a wheelchair. His face was white as the newly fallen snow, and I was tempted to suggest that she put *him* in the wheelchair. At this point, I wasn't sure who needed it more—Jacques or me.

"How are we doing?" the nurse said cheerfully as she assisted me out of the car. "Can I get you anything?"

"Starbucks," I said with a groan.

"Excuse me, hon?" she asked, a confused look on her face.

I couldn't explain it myself. Despite the pain and discomfort, I was dying for my favorite drink. "Uh, I don't know. It popped into my head. I'd love a mocha Frappuccino right about now."

"Well, just when I thought I'd heard everything." The nurse grinned as she helped me to my feet.

Jacques was sweating profusely but tried to help. "Cripes. You're not exactly easy to move, my love. Too much Starbucks and whipped cream might have been your downfall."

"That's a low blow," I muttered between my clenched teeth.

The nurse took my pulse and then wheeled me toward the entrance. "When was your last contraction?"

"About a minute ago."

She clucked her tongue against the roof of her mouth in apparent concern as the automatic doors separated upon our arrival. The nurse didn't look much older than Darcy. "Well, that little baby wants to come now, so we'd better get you prepped for the delivery room," she said. "Who's your physician?"

"Dr. Sanchez." I groaned as another contraction started.

"He's on vacation this week, but Dr. Julius is available. She's doing rounds, but we'll get her in to see you right away. Is this your first?"

Jacques, who'd been holding my hand, screeched in sudden pain. "Dear God. She's like a volcano that keeps erupting over and over—ouch!" He went down to one knee. "You're killing me!"

"We'll get your husband fitted into some scrubs so he can help you deliver," the nurse assured me.

"Deliver?" Jacques eyes widened in fright. "I don't want to see that."

The nurse glared at him. "You should have thought of that nine months ago."

"He's not my husband," I protested.

Her face took on an apologetic look. "Well, your partner, then. I shouldn't have made assumptions. My mistake."

"Look here, miss," Jacques huffed as he got to his feet. "This happens to be my best friend."

Her expression was puzzled. "Hey, whatever you want to call her is none of my business. Let's concentrate on bringing your beautiful child into the world for now."

"But it's not my kid," Jacques protested. "And I..." His face turned beet red. "I may not be able to handle this. Uh, I think I might be a bit squeamish."

The look on his face and his statement caused me to start laughing so hard that I couldn't stop. I kept on giggling as the nurse wheeled me into a room in the maternity ward. "Oh, wait till I tell everyone in the office about this."

"Don't you dare!" Jacques gasped.

The nurse handed me an unattractive blue hospital gown with black zig zag decorations on it. "I think you're becoming hysterical. Do you need help getting undressed, hon?"

I glanced up at Jacques, who made a face. "God, don't look at me," he said.

Good grief. I struggled not to roll my eyes. "Can you call Darcy and make sure that she knows to come home for the boys? And try Greg again, please. I've already left him two—" I sucked in some air. "Uh oh. Another one! I need to push!"

The nurse shooed Jacques toward the door. "Why don't you go out to the front desk and give them some information on your...ah...friend. I'll help her with the clothes. What's your name, hon?"

I hated it when people half my age called me hon. "Cindy. Cindy York."

"Thank God," Jacques breathed. He couldn't scurry out the door fast enough.

"I'm Betsy," the nurse said. As she helped me get out of my clothes and into the gown, I felt totally helpless and bigger than a Volkswagen. I was past caring at this point, though. All I wanted was for the pain to be over and to have Greg at my side.

Betsy placed my clothes on a nearby counter. "I'll be right back. Let me go check and see where the doctor is." She hummed a little tune low in her throat as she closed the door behind her. I remained in the wheelchair even though the bed was only a couple of feet away. Betsy must not have wanted to attempt to get me into it by herself. Maybe she'd gone off in search of a forklift.

Betsy was back within a few minutes with a young Hispanic woman who beamed at me with dark intelligent eyes. Her hand was soft and cool to the touch. "I'm Dr. Julius, Cindy. The anesthesiologist will be here in a minute. I've been reviewing your chart."

"Anesth—" I couldn't even say the entire word without stopping for breath. "Why? What's going on?"

She and Betsy both helped me into the delivery bed, and to their credit, neither one of them grunted at the exertion—much. "Since your last birth was by C-section, I think we need to prep you for an emergency one right away."

"But the baby's coming now!" I protested. "I need to push."

"Well, try not to do that," Betsy warned.

Dr. Julius shot her a strange look and then turned her attention back to me. "The ultrasound technician will be in shortly. I want her to do a quick scan to make sure that the baby isn't in any imminent danger."

As if on cue, there was a tap on the door and a heavyset woman with short red hair wheeled the machine in. "Hi there," she said cheerfully. "Is this Mrs. York?"

I barely managed to nod as another contraction hit me.

"I'm Gina. I know you're uncomfortable, so I'll be as quick as I can." She moved my gown apart and squirted some lubricating gel on my stomach. It was cold, and I winced from the contact. Gina glided the transducer back and forth while staring at the screen. I looked too but couldn't tell what she was seeing.

"Is the baby okay?" I asked nervously.

Dr. Julius peered over the tech's shoulder while she printed out a few pictures. "The baby looks fine, Cindy, but she's transverse. We'll have to do an emergency C-section right away. You probably wanted a natural birth, but I'm afraid that won't be possible."

"It's fine, really." The contractions were already wearing me out, so the thought of pushing for another hour or more didn't hold much appeal. "I've done both, so it doesn't matter to me. I only want my husband."

"Good luck." Gina smiled. She left the photos on the table by the bed and wheeled the machine out of the room, almost crashing into Jacques as he rushed through the doorway.

Jacques was followed by a tall man who wore a set of scrubs identical to his. "I'm Dr. Gordon, Cindy. Any changes in allergies or medications since your last pregnancy?"

I shook my head. "Everything is the same, except that I'm a good deal older."

He gave a deep, throaty, contagious laugh. "Well, at least you still have your sense of humor."

"Oh wonderful." Dr. Julius smiled at Jacques. "Your husband made it after all."

Betsy snorted. "He's not her husband. They're just *friends*."

Oh, good grief. There was no time or energy left for me to attempt to explain this again. I stared up at Jacques, who looked like he was about to rupture something. "Did you get ahold of Greg?"

He nodded. "He's on his way, and Darcy will be home right after school to look after the rug rats. Greg said he'd call his mother and ask her to stay with the kids tonight."

Ugh. Helen York feeding my kids spaghetti and barbs. I didn't have much choice in the matter so might as well try to make the best of it.

"Aren't you her partner?" Dr. Gordon asked Jacques.

Jacques shook his head. "No, but I'm ready to stand in for him." He stood tall and erect as Betsy handed him a surgical mask. "I won't let you go through this alone, Cin."

I stopped panting for a moment and watched him. Although I appreciated Jacques' loyalty, I didn't have the heart to tell him it might be easier for me to go this alone than be accompanied by him to the operating room. Something told me that Jacques might have more trouble than me getting through the actual delivery part.

The anesthesiologist gave me a shot before they lifted the sides of the bed, and then we were on our way to the delivery room.

Jacques reached for my hand as he trotted by my side. "Nothing to worry about, darling. Nothing at all." He was breathing too heavily.

The shot was working quickly because Jacques and the room were turning a bit hazy. "You're green." Or at least I thought so.

"Fine," he gasped. "Never better. Hey, I once saved you from a psychopathic killer, remember? Shoot, this will be nothing. Nothing at all."

Dr. Julius and Betsy both glanced at him in bewilderment, but neither one commented. Maybe they thought he was hallucinating.

"Did he get a shot as well?" I joked to the anesthesiologist. Suddenly I was pain free and loving it. With any luck I'd be holding my little girl soon, and I couldn't wait to see her. Then Percy's face flashed before my eyes, and I shuddered. "He said he knew."

"What, darling?" Jacques puffed as we went through the doors of the operating room. He bent closer so that his ear was next to my mouth. "Who said what?"

"Percy said he knew who killed his...wife...Vanessa. That he was killed the same way she'd been." I started to shake. "Cold. I'm freezing."

Jacques frowned. "What are you trying to say, Cin?"

"Please," Betsy called over as she washed her hands in a nearby sink. "This is hardly the time for Mrs. York to be talking about such unpleasant subjects. She's about to have a baby!"

Another nurse hung a sterile blue drape in front of me so that I wouldn't be able to see the actual surgery. Betsy came over to assist her.

"He didn't do it," I said.

Jacques sandwiched my hand between both of his. "Darling, you shouldn't be thinking about that right now. My God, your hands are ice cold." He turned to Betsy, who was adjusting her mask. "Can Cindy have another blanket, or does she need to pay extra for it?"

"You need to move up next to Mrs. York," Dr. Gordon told him. "Unless you're not planning on staying for the operation."

"I'm here for the duration." Jacques swallowed hard and then smiled nervously down at me. "There's no way you'll get me out of here."

The door of the delivery room was pushed open, and Greg

rushed in, his blue eyes wide with alarm as they settled on me. Jacques released my hand and moved aside.

"Thank God." Jacques clasped his hands together as if in prayer. "I don't think I could have made it."

Greg pushed the hair back from my face and kissed me gently on the lips. "Are you all right? What happened, sweetheart?" He stared from me to Jacques in confusion.

"Are you her husband or another *friend*?" Betsy quipped.

Greg frowned at the nurse. "I'm Cindy's husband." He turned back to me. "How'd you go into labor? Did you fall in the snow?"

"Worse," Jacques muttered. "She found a dead body."

Greg's face was thunderstruck. "What?"

"Mr. York," Dr. Julius said. "If you plan on staying for the operation, you need to put on scrubs and a surgical mask."

"Of course I'm staying." Greg let go of my hand to put the scrubs on and then washed his hands in the sink, all the while keeping his eyes pinned on me. He must have been wondering how I'd managed to encounter yet another dead body. This was becoming the norm for me.

"Feeling anything, Mrs. York?" Dr. Gordon stood behind me, his hand resting lightly on my head.

I gave him a thumbs-up. "Totally numb and loving it."

Jacques came over and kissed me on the forehead. "I'll be in the waiting room. Good luck, darling. Soon you'll have a new little princess to love," he said tenderly.

"Thanks for bringing her." Greg reached for my hand again.

"Beautiful cut, doctor," Betsy said from the other side of the drape. I couldn't see anything from my position in the bed, except for Greg and Dr. Gordon, who was standing behind us. My only disappointment with the C-section was that it meant a longer recovery, but the baby's health was more important. After the twins I'd been up and around within a week, so hopefully that would be the case this time. I kept trying to focus on the joy of the situation, but Percy's face would not leave my mind.

Another nurse's voice sounded from somewhat far away. "Mr. Forte, there's a policeman out in the hall who wants to speak to you."

"I'll be right there," Jacques told her.

"Are you ready to meet your daughter, Cindy?" Dr. Julius's voice filled the room.

I was aware of a tugging sensation in my abdomen but nothing more. Greg brought my hand to his mouth and kissed it. "She'll be here soon, sweetheart. You're doing great."

Jacques, who had disappeared from my sight, suddenly let out a blood-curdling shriek. It was followed by a loud thud then silence that emanated throughout the room.

Betsy's voice was full of disbelief. "You've got to be kidding me."

Panic set in. "What's wrong? Is the baby okay?"

"I've got this," the second nurse said. "He seems to be coming around."

"He? The baby's a girl," I said, confused. "Will someone please tell me what's going on?"

"Everything's fine," Greg assured me.

Dr. Julius's rich voice came from the other side of the curtain and spoke in a soothing tone. "There's nothing to worry about, Cindy. We'll have your daughter out in a jiffy. Everything looks great except for your—ah, friend. He seems to have passed out."

CHAPTER FIVE

Greg placed a soft kiss on my lips. "You were incredible, sweetheart." He sat next to my bed and held our sleeping daughter in his arms, staring down at her in wonder. "She's as beautiful as her mother."

As I watched the two of them together, I decided that life couldn't get much better. If only we could stay like this forever. I was drowsy from the medication and wanted to sleep but didn't want to miss a minute of this special time.

I had memories of Greg holding all of our newborn children in a similar manner—Darcy, our eldest, when he'd been puffed up with pride at the brand-new feeling of fatherhood. He'd cradled the twins, one in each arm, and had been filled with the incredulity of how our family had suddenly managed to double in size. This time he was an old hand at it, a bona fide pro. The soft glow in his eyes as he looked at his daughter managed to bring tears to my own.

The morphine had helped with the pain, but I tried not to move around much. I'd already nursed the baby once, and she'd had no issues, which was a relief. She was six pounds and two ounces of pure beauty—not a bad weight for a baby that was a month early. She was also in perfect health, and I sent a small prayer of thanks up for that.

"She needs a name," I reminded Greg.

"I'm working on it." He grinned.

The baby made a tiny whimper, as if to say she'd prefer one too. My heart overflowed with loved whenever I looked at her. Even though she was my fourth child, that feeling of awe that Greg and I had made this perfect little person still managed to blow me away. This was also a bittersweet time because I knew with certainty she'd be my last baby as well. We had decided not to tempt fate again, and Greg had gone in for a vasectomy last month.

The trauma and discomfort were all but forgotten now—the endless morning sickness, various body part swelling, depression, and the initial shock when I'd first discovered I was pregnant. She'd only been here for an hour, and already I couldn't imagine life without her. "We have so much to be thankful for."

Greg kissed me again. "What do you think about Grace for a name?"

I considered it for a minute. In lieu of everything that had happened in the past eight months, it seemed a perfect choice. Plus, I liked the fact that the first letter of her name linked Grace with her father's. "Sounds like we have a winner."

Grace's hair was a light brown like Greg's, but her eyes were my hazel color and not her father's blue, to my disappointment. Still, they were enormous in size and beautiful, with green pupils and a goldish brown color around the outside edges. When she opened them for a split second, I was mesmerized. "Oh, she's so perfect, isn't she?"

Greg kissed her little fingers. "As pretty as her mommy. It looks like she has your mother's nose, doesn't it?"

"Yes." Greg had never met my mother but had seen numerous pictures of her. She'd died from breast cancer before Greg and I met. It made me sad that she'd never had a chance to know him or her grandchildren. It was one thing that I truly regretted. "She would have loved Grace."

He smiled, but his expression was guarded. "I know why you went into labor early. Because you found that guy—the killer. Percy, right? Jacques told me all about it when you were in recovery."

With a sigh, I lay back among the pillows. "We don't know that for sure. I'd been having brutal back pain for a while. That could have been a sign too." But I couldn't ignore what he was saying—the doctor herself had said that stress might have brought on the early labor. "We can't be positive that Percy was a killer."

Greg watched me sharply. "What *are* you trying to say?"

At that moment, someone knocked on my door, and Jacques poked his head in. "Feeling up to some company?"

"Absolutely." I beamed. "Come in and meet our daughter."

As Jacques approached the bed, I was shocked by the sight of him. His suit coat was wrinkled, his glasses crooked, and he had a white, square bandage on his forehead. So much for the sharply dressed, self-assured man today.

"Are you sure you're okay?" he asked.

I stared at him. "Probably in better shape than you."

Jacques flushed as he gave me a kiss on the cheek and placed a vase of red roses on the table next to me. "From the gift shop downstairs. And I'm fine. The doctor said it's only a slight concussion."

Greg stared down at Grace in his arms, so it was difficult to see his face, but I did catch the sly smile quiver at the corners of his mouth. Apparently, so did Jacques. He puffed out his chest in response. "Well, excuse me. If I wanted to see a woman giving birth, I would have married one."

Greg lost it then and started to laugh, his body movement stirring the baby during her sound sleep.

I held out my arms. "Give her to me. I need to nurse her again soon anyway."

Jacques' face went white and I was quick to reassure him. "Don't worry. I'll wait until you leave. I'd prefer not to see you faint again."

Greg snorted back a laugh as he handed Grace over to me.

"Okay, smart aleck. Why don't you tell Jacques about what happened when I went to the hospital to have Darcy?" I asked smugly.

The smile faded from my husband's lips. "I don't remember."

"Oh?" I held the baby against my chest. "You don't remember telling the nurse that you thought you were having morning sickness too?"

"Hey, give me a break. It was my first kid," Greg complained.

"Mine too," Jacques said wearily as he came to the side of my bed and gently touched the baby's tiny hand. "She's beautiful, Cin. What's her name?"

"Grace." I glanced at Greg. "Maybe Grace Jacquelyn?"

We had discussed Jacquelyn as a possible middle name before, but I'd never informed Jacques about it. Since Greg didn't like the name Eileen and I didn't want Helen, it seemed to be the next logical choice.

Greg nodded in approval. "I like it."

Jacques' mouth dropped open in amazement. "Wow, I'm so honored. But why me?"

I shifted the baby in my arms. "Why *not* you? You're family to us. After everything you've done for me, it seemed appropriate."

Jacques didn't get emotional often, but his green eyes misted over at that moment. "Thank you."

"We'd also like you and Ed to be godparents," Greg put in.

He said nothing for a moment as he stood there, squeezing my hand. "Well, I'm definitely in. As for Ed, I—I uh, don't know where things stand right now." Jacques cleared his throat and changed the subject. "I gave a statement to a cop in the waiting room. He mentioned wanting to speak to you as well and asked one of the nurses for your room number. He got a call right after we finished up, but I assume he'll be in here shortly."

Greg's face was solemn. "What'd you tell him?"

Jacques bit into his lower lip. "I said that I heard Cindy screaming and ran into the house. Then I called 9-1-1 and, as soon as the police arrived, took Cindy to the hospital."

"I'm glad you were with her," Greg said. "I'd hate to think what might have happened if she'd been all alone in that killer's house when she went into labor."

I laid the baby down in bed next to me, fighting my sleepy state again. "Don't say that, Greg."

He drew his eyebrows together. "Don't say what?"

"About Percy. I don't believe he killed his wife," I said emphatically. "I think he was framed. The last thing he said to me when he was dying was, 'Find killer.'"

"So you think he knew who the killer was?" Jacques asked.

I nodded. "Maybe the same person who killed Percy's wife killed him. The cause of his death was identical to hers—they both had their throats cut. Percy told me that he loved Vanessa and he never would have hurt her. Why bother to say that in his dying hour? Wouldn't that be the time for a confession?"

Before either man could reply, another tap sounded on my door. A policeman in a dark blue uniformed jacket looked in at us. "Mrs. York? I'm Officer Henderson. I wonder if I could ask you a few questions."

Greg stood to his full six-foot height and addressed the man. "My wife just had a baby, officer. She really needs her rest."

I placed a hand on his arm. "It's all right." The baby was sleeping, and we might as well get it over with. Hopefully then we could put this horrible incident behind us.

Officer Henderson was as tall as Greg, with a burly looking physique and a mass of carrot-colored hair that surprised me when he took his hat off. "It won't take long. I promise." He reached into the breast pocket of his coat for a pad and pen. "I was talking to your boss." He motioned toward Jacques. "He informed me that you were the one to find Mr. Rodgers?"

"That's right. He'd been stabbed—his throat cut." My eyelids were growing heavy again, so I sat straight up in the bed. "He was trying to tell me who did this to him but died before he could get the words out."

Sensing that I was tired, Greg picked the baby up off the bed next to me and sat back down in the chair with her in his arms.

"You didn't see his assailant or anything suspicious?" Officer Henderson asked.

"No, sir. All I remember was Percy lying on the floor. There was blood…lots of blood."

Greg drew the blanket closer around Grace. "Can't we do this some other time? I think my wife has been upset enough for one day. Finding Mr. Rodgers like that sent her into premature labor."

The man looked sheepish. "I understand that, but if we're going to catch this person, it's imperative to get all the details as soon as possible." He turned his attention back to me. "You didn't notice anything unusual about the body or anything significant?"

Unsure what he was getting at, I scrunched my face up tightly and tried to remember the specific details. "No, I don't think so."

He reached into his breast pocket again and drew out my key ring, which was in a plastic bag. "Is this yours?"

I hadn't even realized it was missing. "Oh yes. They must have fallen out of my pocket when I found Percy."

Officer Henderson didn't reply. Instead, he reached into his pocket again. *How many goodies does he have in there?* He drew out another plastic bag with a weird-looking playing card inside. "Did you happen to drop this as well?"

I reached out my hand for the bag and examined the card. It

was brown in color and appeared to be quite old. There was a man in ragged clothes featured on the face of it. He was without shoes and wearing a floral-patterned outfit. The man carried a stick on his back and held what appeared to be feathers in his hand. "No, I've never seen it before."

Jacques leaned over for a better look at the card. "That's a tarot card."

Officer Henderson nodded. "Correct. It doesn't belong to either one of you?"

Jacques shook his head. "Not mine. Was it found on Mr. Rodgers?"

The policeman acted uncomfortable as he nodded. "It was next to his body. You might not have seen it, Mrs. York, when you found Mr. Rodgers, because his body may have been blocking it from your view. We found it underneath him."

Greg leaned forward in the chair. "Do you think the killer left it as some type of message?"

"I really can't comment any further," Officer Henderson hedged. "We can't even be positive that the killer's the one who left it. I wanted to make sure that it didn't belong to either one of you first."

"Do you have any leads?" I asked.

Officer Henderson's face colored a bit, and he avoided a direct answer to my question. "The man was a convicted killer, so there may have been several people who wanted him dead. We're looking at several possibilities." This was his veiled way of informing us that the police did not plan to share any information with us. "It could have been a case of suicide as well. But I'm glad that you and your baby are okay, Mrs. York."

"Wait a minute." I held up a hand. "This might sound crazy to you, but I don't think Mr. Rodgers killed his wife or himself for that matter. He was trying to tell me who stabbed him, and I believe it's the same person who killed his wife."

Officer Henderson gave me a dubious look then tipped his

hat at me. "Well, everyone is entitled to their own opinion, ma'am." His tone reeked of sarcasm, and I wasn't amused. Before I could say anything further, he gave us all a quick wave and closed the door quietly behind him.

"Wow," Jacques breathed. "It's like he didn't even care about the guy's murder. Maybe they feel Percy got exactly what he deserved or even that he killed himself out of guilt or something."

The thought had crossed my mind too. I didn't like this scenario, but what could I do about it? The man was already dead, plus I had no ties to him. The baby started to fuss and opened her mouth. "I need to feed her."

Jacques got up instantly and kissed me. "I'll go over to your house and bring the kids by to meet their sister."

"That's so sweet of you. We appreciate that," I said. "Thanks for everything."

"I'll walk out with you," Greg offered. He turned back and blew me a kiss. "Oh, remind me when I get back that I need to tell you something about my mother."

His words filled me with shining hope. Maybe she fell off her broomstick? *Not nice, Cindy.* As I began to nurse the baby, I was instantly ashamed of my feelings. Yes, Helen York had never liked me and enjoyed giving me a hard time, but she was wonderful to my kids and had already bought the baby several items of clothing plus a new car seat and playpen, since we no longer had any of the items that Stevie and Seth had previously used. I gently stroked Grace's cheek as she ate. I was filled with happiness today and prepared to sprinkle some on Helen as well.

My hospital phone rang from the small table next to me. I was close enough to grab it without disturbing the baby. "Hello?"

"Oh hello, Cindy," Helen York's lukewarm voice greeted me.

Speak of the pitchfork-toting devil. *Think nice thoughts now.* "Hello, Helen."

"How's the baby?" she asked.

I stared down at the perfect little angel in my arms, and joy emanated from my voice. "She's wonderful. Thanks for taking care of the kids."

Helen ignored my comment. "Is my son there?"

"No, he stepped out for a second. Would you like me to have him call you when he gets back?"

"It's not necessary. Tell him that I brought the rest of my things over. I'll make myself comfortable in the study. There's no need for me to move into Darcy's room and disturb her."

I drew my eyebrows together in confusion. "Well, that's nice of you, but it's only for one night. Greg will be back tomorrow."

She gave a mirthful laugh. "Oh, apparently he hasn't told you yet."

An uneasy feeling swept over me. "Told me what?"

Annoyance crept into Helen's voice. "About my roof, of course! Part of it fell in this morning, and the repair will take a couple of weeks. I told Gregory that I'd be moving in with you until it's fixed."

CHAPTER SIX

"Why can't we have Captain Crunch for breakfast every day like Tyler does?" Stevie asked. "He said his mom lets him eat Reese's Puffs cereal too."

"Because there's too much sugar in it." Greg's tired voice floated up the stairs to me from the kitchen. "Now hurry up and eat your Pop-Tart before the bus gets here."

Good grief. I descended the staircase slowly and walked in the direction of the kitchen. Today marked ten days since the baby's birth. My pain from the surgery had subsided, but I was still a bit sore and tired easily, especially from nursing the baby every three to four hours. The doctor didn't want me driving for at least a couple of more days, and Grace had her first checkup with the pediatrician this afternoon. Greg was taking a long lunch from work so that he could drive us there.

Helen had gone home for the morning to talk with the contractor who was fixing her roof. I'd hoped she would have returned home by now, but no such luck. We'd had a significant snowfall the last couple of days, and much to my chagrin, that hadn't helped with the progress.

Greg had insisted on getting the twins up and breakfast ready, with Darcy's reluctant assistance. To his credit, Greg had told his mother that the decision about her moving in with us was entirely up to me, and I appreciated that. Regardless, Helen always did and said as she pleased and already had her things moved in when she'd called me at the hospital. Since Greg had no vacation time left until April and "some goings on" at work that he wouldn't elaborate about, I'd caved. It was nice to have someone helping with the household chores and making sure that the kids ate things other than Pop-Tarts, but it also came at a price. A Wicked Witch of the West–sized sales tag.

The baby was sleeping, and Greg had told me to stay in bed and rest, but I felt guilty letting him handle it all. From the sound of things, he was a bit overwhelmed. Plus I knew he had a crucial meeting with a vendor first thing this morning. Greg's job as a salesman for a local auto supply company was hectic and far from glamorous, but most of the time he enjoyed it. It also afforded him the opportunity to work from home occasionally, which was a great help if I had to show a house with little notice.

From the way today was shaping up, maybe I should have stayed in bed. The outdoors was blanketed in snow and made me yearn for springtime. The baby had fussed all night and managed to keep both Greg and me awake. She'd also woken Darcy, who had an important test at school today. She sat at the kitchen table now, her textbook open in front of her.

"Can't you manage to keep my sister quiet?" Darcy demanded, glaring at me with huge dark eyes. "Thanks to her, I got no sleep and am probably going to flunk my Chemistry exam today."

I shuffled over to the coffee pot and poured myself a cup. "I'm sorry, honey. If it makes you feel any better, none of us got any sleep."

"Sweetheart, what are you doing up?" Greg was starting to assemble the twins' lunches and making a mess of the entire counter in the process. "You're supposed to be resting."

I gave him a swift kiss. "Let me do that. You'll be late."

"I slept great," Seth said to Darcy with a mouth full of strawberry Pop-Tart.

Darcy tossed her long dark hair over her shoulder and gave her best murderous stare. "If I'm going to get into a good college or have any chance at a scholarship, I need to do well this year in all of my subjects. Your junior year grades are the ones that all the colleges look at."

"Yes, I'm aware of that." I handed Seth his lunch.

Greg gave his daughter an irritated look. "I thought you'd gotten over this self-absorbed stage of yours. You knew that we'd all need to make adjustments when the baby got here. Where is this coming from?"

"Oh whatever," she grumbled. "I guess I'll suffer through, as usual."

A car horn beeped from outside, and she got to her feet. "That's Jill. She's giving me a ride today."

"Didn't she only get her license a few weeks ago?" I asked in surprise.

"Yeah." Darcy gave a toss of her head as she put her jacket on. "Her parents bought her a new car for her birthday. A Honda Accord. Some people have all the luck *and* money, I guess."

She slammed the kitchen door without another word.

Greg clenched his fists at his side. "I'll talk to her when she gets home. I don't know where this attitude of hers is coming from, but I want it to stop."

"Let it go." I handed Stevie his lunch and started to clear the table. "It's normal with the new baby. Darcy probably feels a bit jealous, but she'll come around." To tell the truth, I was a little disheartened to see her acting like this but tried to dismiss it.

Darcy and I had experienced a near brush with death last summer, and since then, we'd been closer than ever. She'd been wonderfully supportive during the pregnancy and had babysat the boys countless times without complaint. She'd even helped me Christmas shop for them. "Then again, something else might be bothering her."

"Bradley Sherman asked somebody else to the prom already," Seth volunteered. "I bet that's what she's mad about."

This was news to me. Bradley was a senior who'd recently taken Darcy to a Christmas dance, and I knew how much she liked him. "How'd you know this?"

The bus honked from outside, and Seth raced to the door. "See you later, Mom!"

"Hold on a minute." Greg reached over and grabbed him by the backpack. "Answer your mother. The bus will wait for a few seconds."

Stevie giggled. "Seth was listening. If he presses a glass to the wall, he can hear everything Darcy says on the phone to her dumb friends. What color bra should I buy? Do you think that cute guy is going out with anyone? All lame stuff."

"He's making that up!" Seth protested.

I narrowed my eyes. "I'd better not hear about you doing that again."

"When do I get to go to a prom?" Stevie asked as they went out the kitchen door together and down the path Greg had shoveled earlier.

"No girl would ask you," Seth retorted. "But maybe Rusty will take you."

Rusty, our golden retriever, had been led out to his pen in the yard a little while ago. At the mention of his name, he perked his ears up and watched the boys get on the bus while letting out a pitiful whimper.

Greg waited until they got on the bus then shut the door.

"Seth and that inquisitive nature of his. He must get it from you."

"Very funny." So far, the boys hadn't heard about my latest encounter with a dead body, and I planned to keep it that way. The twins enjoyed regaling their classmates with details of how their mother had sent a murderer to jail last summer. Their teacher had even called me herself, worried that the twins had an overactive imagination. Imagine my discomfort when I'd had to assure her the stories were true.

Greg picked up his briefcase and coat and pulled me close to him. "Will you and the baby be okay until I get back?"

"We'll be fine." I placed my arms around his neck as his lips closed over mine. "But I'm so glad you're coming with us. It will be nice to have you there, and then you can see how Grace has grown too."

He gazed at me worriedly. "I wish I could stay home with you for the morning, but I have that blasted meeting."

"We'll be fine," I assured him and adjusted the collar on his overcoat. "Please don't worry."

He stroked my cheek softly. "I'll always worry. I happen to love you more than anything. Try to get some rest, baby. If you need anything in the meantime, call Mom."

Uh thanks, but no thanks. "How—" I hated to ask this. "How much longer until her roof is done?"

Greg's mouth crinkled into a smile. "Hopefully not more than another week. You overheard what she said last night, didn't you?"

"How could I not?" I clenched my fists into balls as her words carried back to me. "'That baby looks exactly like your UPS man,'" I mimicked. "'You'd better watch out, Gregory.'"

Greg had laughed it off last night and told his mother that if I overheard, she'd might as well start packing now. They'd been in the kitchen, and I'd been about to confront her, but Grace had started crying, so I'd headed back upstairs. As I'd nursed her

I sat and stewed about what to say to the woman. One more dig like that, and my hands might find their way around my pretentious mother-in-law's throat.

"It's a good thing for her that the kids didn't hear," I said tartly. "Let's face it, Greg. She's never liked me, and I'm not thrilled about having her here. Has she been helpful? Absolutely, but at what cost?"

He sighed heavily. "I don't know what her problem is, Cin. If it makes you feel any better, she never liked anyone I dated before you."

"But I'm your wife, and we've been married over 18 years. Isn't it about time she cut me a little slack?"

Greg nodded. "You're absolutely right. Would you like me to have a talk with her?"

"No. But I'm warning you—next time I'm going to let her have it." My fists were still clenched at my sides.

He kissed me again. "Whatever you say, Rocky Balboa. You're the boss. I'll grab Rusty and bring him in for you."

"Thanks. See you about noon." I opened the door.

Greg gave me a saucy grin. "Think kind thoughts now." He was back in a minute with the dog, blew me a kiss, and then took off. I stood in the doorway, despite the cold, and watched him drive off, mulling his comment over in my head.

If I could only manage to ignore the snarky remarks that flew out of Helen's mouth, there might be a slim chance that I wouldn't kill her before the roof was finished. While I was in the hospital, she'd cleaned the house from top to bottom and even frozen several meals in the freezer. Perhaps I should be grateful, but the woman had an ulterior motive for everything she did, and after the UPS man comment, she was skating on thin ice with me.

I checked in on Grace, who was still sleeping, and thought I might catch a quick nap as well but first decided to throw some laundry into the wash and change the sheets in the twins' room.

I had gone downstairs to the kitchen for another cup of decaf coffee when my cell phone buzzed from the counter. It was a local number and one I didn't recognize. There was no way I was showing anyone a house today but still couldn't resist picking up the call. "Cindy York. May I help you?"

"Hello, Ms. York," a deep, ethereal female voice greeted me on the other end. "My name is Eleanor Cassidy. I was a close friend of Stella Rodgers."

The name didn't register right away. "I'm sorry. You must have me mixed up with someone else. Is this about a house?"

"Sort of." The woman paused for a moment. "Stella was the owner of the mansion at 25 Rodgers Way until she passed away last year. I believe you contracted for the listing recently?"

"Oh!" Heat rose through my face. "Please excuse me. I had a baby last week, and my brain is a little slow on the uptake today."

"Congratulations." There was silence again. "I'm sorry to be calling you at such an inconvenient time. Maybe you'd rather refer me to someone else."

"Are you looking for a house?" If so, I'd send her to Jacques. I didn't have the energy to look through a bunch of listings and take her to showings all day. Besides, I couldn't be away for the baby for long periods of time.

"Not exactly." Eleanor was silent for a beat. "You see, I was Stella's best friend. We'd known each other since we were children. I was her maid of honor when she married Simon. It was stipulated in Stella's will that if her grandson should pass on, I would take over the house. So, it appears that I am now the new legal owner of 25 Rodgers Way. When I was there last night, I saw your card on the desk. It was the same desk that they found Percy—" Her voice trailed off. "Anyway, I was wondering if I could possibly talk to you about representation."

This was the last thing I'd expected. "Uh, Mrs. Cassidy, I uh—"

"It's Miss," she interrupted.

"My apologies, but I'm not sure this is a good idea. You may not know all the details of Percy's death, but I was the one to find his body. I decided not to take the listing and had gone over to the house to give him his release."

"Yes, I did know that," Eleanor said quietly. "The police told me that a real estate agent found him. They didn't identify you by name, but I kind of put two and two together from the business card. Percy never signed the release form though, correct? I couldn't find one anywhere."

Immediately, I was on the defensive and sat down at the kitchen table, my hands wrapped around the coffee mug for warmth. "No, he didn't, but that doesn't matter. His death terminates any listing agreement we might have had, Miss Cassidy. It doesn't matter that he never actually signed it."

"Perhaps," she said. "But you see, I don't have any intention of residing in that house. I've been living in California for the past twenty years and am very happy there. You can imagine my surprise the other day when Stella's attorney called and told me about Percy."

"Did you know about the clause in Stella's will beforehand?" I asked.

"Of course," she said. "Everyone knew when they gathered for the reading last fall." She paused. "Mrs. York, err—can I call you Cindy?"

"Please."

"I'd like for you to call me Eleanor." She hesitated for a moment. "Will you be attending Percy's wake this afternoon?"

"To be honest, I didn't even know about it." My mind had been on other things for the past week, and there hadn't been time to look at a newspaper or watch television. When I had let my mind wander briefly in that direction, I'd assumed that Percy had been laid to rest already. The police had not questioned me since the day in the hospital, so I'd also assumed they were not seriously looking at me as a suspect. That was a welcome change. "I thought the funeral would have been held by now."

"No. We had to wait for the coroner to release the body."

I'd forgotten about that procedure. "Oh, right. What time is it being held?"

"From three to seven at McBride and Tate Funeral Home." Eleanor lowered her voice. "I would love a chance to talk to you about the house—and other things."

The hair rose on the back of my neck. "What other things?"

She cleared her throat. "I wondered if Percy told you anything about his wife's murder. I'm guessing that's why you opted out of the contract, because you heard that he'd recently gotten out of prison."

I had to be careful about what I said. "The reasons are private between the client and real estate agent, so I'm afraid I can't divulge them. But I will tell you that it wasn't a good time for me to list the house."

"Right," she said in a somewhat sarcastic tone. "Anyway, I'm interested in unloading the property as soon as possible, and since you had the listing before, I thought I could possibly entice you with the sale and assure you that *I* am not a murderer."

Oh brother. Embarrassment heated my face, and I was relieved she couldn't see it. "I'm sure you're not Eleanor, but that's not why—"

"Please," she implored. "Can you at least meet me at the funeral home, and we'll talk then? About four o'clock, maybe?"

She was making it difficult for me to say no. Grace's appointment was at one, so that should give me plenty of time. "I—I really can't—"

"It won't take long," she assured me. "This would mean so much to me. I want to get all the affairs in order and get back to California as soon as possible. I—I'm afraid to be here."

Now we were getting to the truth of the matter. An uneasy feeling of dread swept over me. "Eleanor, there's something that you're not telling me. Do you know who could have killed Percy?"

Her voice shook. "No, but someone definitely wants that house. In fact, they want it enough to kill for it."

CHAPTER SEVEN

"Will you be back in time for dinner, or should I go ahead and make it?" my mother-in-law asked.

I put a finger to my lips. Grace had just finished nursing, and I was in the process of laying her down in the crib. Greg drove us home from the doctor and had already returned to work. Without a word to my mother-in-law, I crept quietly toward the door and down the stairs with her following, like a cat waiting to pounce on a mouse. She did it so well.

Jacques liked to refer to Helen as "the mother-in-law who came airmailed straight from hell." Helen York didn't look like the devil though. She's a sophisticated, attractive woman in her late sixties or early seventies with short gray hair perfectly coiffed and piercing blue eyes that aren't as soft or as warm as her son's. She never divulges her true age to anyone, and even Greg has admitted he isn't positive how old she is.

Since day one, Helen has never been a fan of mine, but we'd learned to stay out of each other's way—well, until we wound up living together, that is. I was still smarting from the UPS remark but chose not to bring it up. I was saving it as ammunition for another day.

I placed my cell phone in my purse and checked my watch. Three thirty. Jacques was due any minute. When I'd told him about the phone call from Eleanor, he had practically begged to come along. This was fine with me, especially since I was supposed to limit my driving for a couple of more days.

"Cynthia, you did not answer my question," Helen said in that condescending tone she always liked to use with me. "Why don't I go ahead and make dinner, in case you get held up?"

I tried to think. Grace would need to eat again as soon I got home. "Okay, that's fine. Thank you."

"This way you can concentrate on feeding the baby when you get back," Helen assured me as she emptied clean cups from the dishwasher and placed them in the kitchen cabinet. That was when I noticed that she had rearranged everything inside them. I gritted my teeth but said nothing.

"Not to worry—I'll make my son and grandchildren a meal they'll never forget. It's about time they ate something besides prefabbed food."

I sucked in some air. *It's only for a few more days.* "Helen, I don't cook prefabbed food." Okay, occasionally if time was an issue, but who didn't do it these days? Most women worked or were too busy caring for their children to make a meal from scratch every night. Helen acted as if I was feeding my family straight from the garbage can.

She tossed her head and ignored my comment as she started to wipe down the countertops. "I can't believe you're going to a wake for that *killer*. Why, that monster of a man sent you into premature labor. We might have lost that darling little angel upstairs."

"Grace is fine." *And thanks for asking about me, by the way.*

Helen snorted. "That flighty boss of yours is driving you?"

Okay, I didn't expect Helen to be concerned about my

welfare. I'd been in the hospital for almost a week, but she had never come to see me, although she had made a visit to the maternity ward. When she had called the hospital looking for Greg, she had never once asked how I was feeling. I could live with that. However, constant jabs and barbs directed at my best friend were not okay. "Jacques is not flighty. He's been going through some difficult situations lately. I'd appreciate it if you'd leave him out of the conversation."

She was obviously gunning for a fight. "Well, I know that he's gay. That's pretty obvious to everyone."

How could this woman be so closed-minded? "What exactly does that mean?"

She prattled on, pretending not to hear me. "From what I understand, he's not a stable businessman either. People say that his sales are flying right out the window."

Anger erupted in my stomach like a volcano. "That's not true. Who told you that?"

Helen straightened up from the dishwasher, surprised at my sharp tone. "There's a real estate agent at my church who mentioned him by name. They said they wouldn't be surprised if he closed up shop soon. You sure know how to pick them, dear."

I folded my arms across my chest. "Excuse me?"

"Your first job was at an agency that tried to frame you for murder," Helen said with a smug smile. "Then you sold a house where a murder happened 25 years ago. If that wasn't enough, now your fruity boss is going to drag you down with him. Thank goodness my son is such a good provider for his family."

The internal reassurances did no good, and I finally snapped. "Wait a minute. This is *my* house, and you will *not* insult me or spew garbage about my boss or anyone else I happen to care about. Do you understand?"

Helen stood there, a cup in one hand, her body frozen in place. She managed a slight nod, her eyes glued to my face.

"You've been very helpful these past few days with the kids and the house," I said calmly. "But as far as I'm concerned, you can go home and sleep in a bedroom full of snow and ice, and it won't hurt my feelings one little bit."

Jacques' car horn tooted from outside. Helen continued to stare at me, open mouthed, while she held fast to my coffee mug in her hand. It had been a Christmas present from the twins that read, "Everything I touch turns to sold." For a second, I thought she might hurl the cup at my head if she managed to unglue her fingers from around it.

"Well, isn't this a fine how do you do," Helen huffed. "Wait until I tell my son."

"Go right ahead." I stuck my arms inside my coat. "For some reason, I don't think you'd want to make him choose between us."

She narrowed her eyes. "You'd better go. Don't keep your little friend waiting."

"You're right. That would be rude. And for the record, I'll take his company over yours any day."

Helen shouted something that sounded like "little witch," but it might have been a word that rhymed with it. I slammed the door behind me, not interested in what else she had to say. My legs were shaking with fury as I got into Jacques' car.

"Nervous?" Jacques asked. "It's only a wake, darling. You've seen one, you've seen them all."

He always had such a way with words. I pulled the seat belt around me. "No, that's not it. I just told my mother-in-law off."

"Get out!" Jacques' tongue was practically hanging out of his mouth as he backed out of the driveway and barely missed the mailbox. "About time. I've been waiting for you to do that ever since we met. How do you feel?"

My body had stopped shaking, and I grinned. "Great, actually. She might poison my dinner tonight, but that's a chance I'll have to take."

He glanced sideways at me. "Something else is bothering you."

I exhaled deeply. "She had some news that you might be interested in." I relayed what Helen had said about his business. "I don't know where she gets these ideas."

Jacques said nothing at first. His mouth had stretched into a taut, thin line. His grip on the steering wheel also tightened as a result. "She's right, you know."

I stared at him in disbelief. "What are you talking about?"

The color rose through Jacques' face. "The main reason our business has dropped is because there's problems with the leads I'm getting. Which means there aren't as many as there used to be. Zoe said the phone barely rings anymore."

Zoe Parker was our new office receptionist. She'd started with us last fall, after our former one, Linda, had left for another position.

"In the rare instance these days that I do get a lead and call on it or distribute it to one of my agents such as yourself, they've already been snapped up by somebody else."

I drew my eyebrows together. "Could there be a leak somewhere? Maybe in our office?"

Jacques' face looked like it had been carved out of stone. "I don't even want to think that someone I employ would do such a thing. Plus, they'd have to go through me to list the home, so how would they manage that?"

"Unless"—I paused for a moment—"they're working with a competitor."

Jacques stopped for a red light and glanced over at me. "Yes, I've thought of that too." His voice was hoarse. "Do you know how much that hurts me?"

Yes, I did know. Jacques had been in business for less than a year, but he always put his employees first. Thanks to the ever-changing market, he'd already seen some tumultuous ups and downs. He didn't deserve to be treated in this manner. If it wasn't for him, I might not even have a job now.

The agency Jacques and I had worked for before, Hospitable Homes, folded last spring due in part to the murder of our co-worker. Jacques had opened his firm afterward and invited all the current agents at Hospitable Homes to join him. His commission split with employees was more than other agencies paid, and he didn't even charge us office fees. Jacques had also thrown a fantastic Christmas party at the local country club and invited our significant others to join us. The thought that someone might be taking advantage of him was enough to make my blood boil.

I laid a hand on his arm. "How are things with Ed?"

Jacques raised his arm as if to stop me from saying anything further. "Nothing's changed." He put his blinker on to go right then turned into the funeral home's parking lot. I was about ready to push him for more information when I caught a look of disbelief on his face. "What's wrong?"

He answered my question with another. "What time do you have?"

"Five minutes after four. Why, what's the matter?"

Jacques glanced around the lot, wide-eyed. "Wow. I thought there might be some type of media circus here, but let me tell you, I certainly did not expect *this.*"

I stared out the window and put a hand to my mouth. There were five cars in the enormous lot, including Jacques' and a hearse. No one likes to think about their own funeral, but I secretly hoped mine would be better attended than Percy's. There wasn't even a news van in sight.

Perhaps it had to do with the articles I'd read online this morning about his murder. Several accounts had called the crime "an eye for an eye" or remarked that he'd done himself in because of the guilt associated with Vanessa's death. The comments I'd read had sickened me. Many of them had been obscene, while others had ranged from "He deserved it" to "I hope he burns in hell for what he did to his wife."

"There's no one here," I said in disbelief as Jacques opened my door and helped me out. "This is awful."

Jacques frowned. "You're looking pale, darling. Are you sure you're feeling up to it? I can handle all the paperwork and talk to Eleanor. If the house sells, you know you'll still get your share."

I hesitated for a moment. "No, I'm all right. The house doesn't worry me. Maybe I feel guilty on some level about Percy. I think he knew his life was in danger and was trying to tell me so. I should have listened."

Jacques looped his arm through mine as we made our way carefully through the parking lot. "Don't blame yourself, love. Anyone else would have done the same thing in your shoes. There's still no proof that he didn't actually kill his wife."

I stared up at the sky, a bleak overcast gray, and noticed that a thick coating of sleet had started to fall. How fitting. What a depressing day to hold a wake. A man who served 20 years for a crime he may not have committed was now dead himself, and the sad part was that no one seemed to care. I had a sudden urge to know more about Percy's stolen life and hoped that the wake would tell us something.

The door was opened by a dark-haired, middle-aged man in a black suit and matching dress shoes that shone like glass. He nodded pleasantly and showed us where to sign the register. Our names were the only ones on the page.

This baffled me. "Are we early?" I whispered.

The man shook his head, a solemn look upon his face. "No, the wake started at three, ma'am. The people in the other room are all family, I believe. How about you?"

"No." What exactly were we to Percy? "We were ah —acquaintances."

Jacques and the man both gave me a blank look, but neither

commented further. Jacques took me by the elbow and guided me toward the viewing room door.

"Nice going. He probably thinks we were his prison mates," Jacques murmured in my ear.

"Well, what did you want me to say?" I whispered back. "That I was his real estate agent until I found out he might be a killer?"

We stood at the back of the room and took in the scene around us. There were five people sitting in chairs in the front row, their backs to us. No one was standing by the coffin. There were no collages of pictures and only one spray of red roses sitting on the coffin. I knew that those had come from Jacques himself because he'd asked my opinion on what to send. As we moved forward, I noticed that heads began to turn and people stared at us in wonder. I wasn't sure why, but it unnerved me.

"You can go first." Jacques nodded toward the kneeler.

I grabbed him by the arm and whispered in his ear. "Are you crazy? You're coming with me."

A muscle ticked in his jaw, but thankfully he didn't argue. We lowered ourselves onto the kneeler, folded our hands in prayer, and stared into Percy's face. In death, the man's coloring was better than it had been while he was alive. This was disturbing. Percy wore a dark blue suit and a matching tie with a white oxford shirt. As I stared down at his hands, I noticed the circle of white skin around the finger on his left hand. Someone had taken his wedding ring off. Had he been wearing one after twenty years? I tried to remember if he'd been wearing it the other day but couldn't be sure.

I must have lost track of time because Jacques elbowed me in the side and stood, helping me along with him. Jacques wasn't very religious, and I knew that funerals made him uncomfortable. I'd been to several wakes in my lifetime, but never any like this. The others had actual mourners in attendance.

A woman with a long white braid hanging over her right shoulder came toward us. She appeared to be in her seventies or so and was dressed in black slacks and an ill-fitting blue blazer. Her face was tanned and leathery looking and immediately made me think of a heavy smoker. When she smiled at us in the depressing atmosphere, it was as if someone had suddenly let in a ray of sunshine. "Are you Cindy York?"

I nodded. "Eleanor?"

She extended her hand. "I'm so glad you could make it." Her large brown eyes shifted toward Jacques with unbridled curiosity. "Are you Cindy's husband?"

Jacques shook his head. "Jacques Forte from Forte Realty. Cindy works for me."

"I'm delighted to meet you both. Come. I'll introduce you to the family." She led the way to the row of people who looked like they wanted to be anywhere else on the face of the earth. She stopped in front of a man with dark brown hair with streaks of silver running through it. "This is Percy's brother, Andrew. Andrew, this is Cindy York and her boss, Jacques, from Forte Realty."

Andrew held out his hand, and I took a moment to study him. He was well built and attractive looking and bore a slight resemblance to Percy. He looked to be in his mid to late forties. "My pleasure," he said politely.

"I'm sorry for your loss," I said.

Andrew waved my comment away with an air of impatience, his dark brown eyes calmly fixated on me. "Thanks, but Percy and I weren't close. If you'll excuse me." He rose to his feet and nodded toward the woman seated next to him. When she didn't immediately move, he cleared his throat noisily. She finally got the message and stood, clutching Andrew by the arm. She was at least ten years younger than her husband and very pretty but in my opinion dressed a bit provocatively for such a solemn affair. Her black dress was too tight and short, with the neckline daringly low. She wore her bleached blonde hair in a bob with pink highlights mixed in. In her presence I began to feel a bit self-conscious, especially because I was still wearing maternity pants since my prepregnancy ones didn't fit yet.

The woman smiled at us pleasantly, but Andrew made no attempt to introduce us. He grabbed her hand as they walked into an adjoining room marked *Private.*

Eleanor watched them leave, her lips pressed tight together in an irritated manner. She then gestured at a woman with curly auburn hair sitting in the seat on the other side of Andrew. Her large blue eyes watched Jacques and me intently while the balding man next to her in a gray suit played on his phone. "This is Percy's sister, Diane Brenner, and her husband, Tom. Diane and Tom, this is the agent I was telling you about, Cindy York. And this is her boss, Jacques Forte of Forte Realty."

Diane rose to shake our hands, while Tom still sat there, texting away. After a sharp look at her husband, he finally sighed and eased himself out of his chair. Tom was a big man—not exactly fat but solid with arms that resembled tree trunks. He towered over the rest of us in height, and I placed him at about six and a half feet.

Diane's red hair set her apart from her brothers. The dusting of freckles on her pert nose gave her face an almost childlike quality, and I guessed she might be the youngest of the three. She glanced around the room nervously and then back at us. "It was good of you both to come."

"We're very sorry for your loss," Jacques murmured as he straightened his tie, a clear indication of his growing discomfort with the situation.

Diane nodded in understanding and then glanced at her husband, who was playing with his phone again. "So, you're the agent Percy mentioned to me." Her eyes rested solemnly on my face. "Percy had only settled in there recently. Do you think the house would have sold?"

I glanced uneasily at Jacques. Now it was my turn to be uncomfortable.

"Ah well, there's a good chance," Jacques admitted. "Like the weather, the market is a bit cold this time of year, and the place needs some work. However, the mansion is a great piece of history in the Saratoga area so—"

"It should have been your house," Tom snarled at his wife with such venom in his voice that Jacques and I both recoiled at his tone. "Percy deserved nothing from that old lady after what he did."

Eleanor's nostrils flared. "You are way out of line, Tom."

"Like hell I am!" Tom exploded. "He slits his wife's throat, and then Diane's senile granny tells him, hey no problem, Percy boy. You can have my house." He gave a loud, throaty laugh. "It's like she was rewarding him for the murder. It makes me freaking sick."

The gentleman who had been at the front door stuck his head in the viewing room. "Is everything okay in here?"

"Tom, please," Diane whispered. "You're making a scene in front of everyone."

Eleanor stared down her nose at Tom. "Stella owed you no explanation for why she did what she did."

Tom snorted. "Sure, you say that now because the place belongs to you. Hell, you're not even family. For the past twenty years you've been off gallivanting in California with your partner. This is such bull—"

"Tom!" Diane's tone was anxious as she reached for his hand. He jerked it away angrily, and she seemed startled by his reaction.

"I've had enough of this crap. Diane, I'm going home. You can hitch a ride back with the new owner of *your* house or one of these other chumps. I'll see you back at our home when this charade is over." Tom cast such a look of intense hatred at both Jacques and me that I practically squirmed with discomfort. He grabbed his coat from the chair he'd been sitting on and strode angrily out of the room.

Diane twisted a handkerchief between her hands. "Please excuse me for a minute," she whispered and trotted out of the room as fast as her kitten heels would carry her.

Eleanor sank down into Diane's discarded chair and patted the one next to her. "Both of you sit down. Take a load off." She rubbed her eyes wearily. "I'm sorry you had to witness that scene. Tom obviously still holds a grudge against Percy. He thinks the house should have been left to Diane."

"Why wasn't it?" I blurted out without thinking. As Greg noted, there was my inquisitive nature at work again.

Eleanor shrugged. "It's hard to say with Stella. Her mind had been fading for several years, but she'd always been close to Percy and me. Stella visited Percy every week in prison—well, up until she got too ill to leave her bed, that is. She never believed that he killed Vanessa, and for the record, neither did I. The rest of the family turned their backs on him, but not me. I never had children or grandchildren of my own, so in a way, Stella's became like mine. But Percy was special." Her lower lip trembled.

"I'm sure he was," I said gently.

Eleanor shrugged. "Who knows what Stella was thinking. Let me tell you, when her grandkids found out about the house during the reading of the will, it didn't exactly go over well."

"That's obvious," Jacques said dryly.

She lowered her voice. "When Tom discovered that Percy was getting the house, he threatened him. Percy was still in prison at the time of the reading. I remember every word Tom said perfectly. He claimed that there was no way Percy would ever take possession of Stella's house. He even—" Uneasily, she stared into my eyes. "He said that he'd see him in hell first."

CHAPTER EIGHT

Jacques and I exchanged a troubled glance. Instinctively, I reached forward and covered the woman's trembling hand with my own and found myself fascinated by the blue transparent veins in hers. For some strange reason, it made me think of my new baby at home and the fragility of life. Overwhelmed, I tried to shake off the sensation. *Focus, Cindy. Focus.* "Do you think that Tom killed Percy?"

Eleanor blinked back a tear. "I don't know. They never got along, but the thought of a family member committing such a heinous crime against another is too much for me to stomach." She straightened up and stared at both of us with a defiant air. "I will tell you this. Percy did *not* kill his wife."

"I don't believe he did either," I added quickly.

Doubt registered in her eyes. "If that's true, then why did you back out of the deal?"

Uneasily, I stared at Jacques. He took off his glasses to polish them with a handkerchief. "Miss Cassidy, we really can't comment on that," he said.

She bit into her lower lip. "I understand. Really, I do. You were a pregnant woman retained by a man who'd recently gotten out of prison for murder."

I tried to change the subject. "When was the last time you talked to Percy?"

She frowned. "A couple of weeks ago, I believe."

"Did he..." I struggled to find the right words. "Did Percy happen to tell you he thought his life might be in danger?"

The color in her cheeks faded. "What are you talking about?"

"The last time I spoke to Percy on the phone—when I said that I had to back out of our agreement—he sounded very strange. He was upset with me for canceling the deal and said something like, 'Maybe we can talk again after your baby's born, if I'm still around.'"

"Was he planning a trip?" Jacques asked.

Eleanor brought a hand to her mouth. "Percy had no money. That's one of the reasons he was selling the house."

"Stella didn't leave him any cash?" I asked.

She shook her head. "I received a small sum, but the brunt of the money went to charities that Stella supported for years. Percy had no intention of remaining in the house, anyway. He also didn't want to be in a town full of people who hated his guts. Percy thought about coming to California to stay with me for a while. He hated the cold weather, and the climate would have been better for his health."

"Did you tell the police this?" I asked.

She forced back a laugh. "It won't do any good, as far as I'm concerned. If you ask me, the cops don't give a damn about Percy's murder. They're convinced it was an eye for an eye type of crime, or maybe they hoped he'd committed suicide. He's already cost taxpayers enough money, so why bother to spend any more investigating his murder?"

"I'm sure that's not true," Jacques said kindly.

She pinned me with her dark, concerned eyes. "Are you going to take the listing or not?"

"Cindy would be delighted," Jacques interrupted.

In shock, I glared at him. "Jacques, I—"

Eleanor rose from her chair. "Excellent. If you'll excuse me for a moment, I need to use the ladies' room. I suspect that's where Diane headed off to, and I would like to have a quick word with her. Do you happen to have a contract with you?"

"I always carry one with me," Jacques said quickly. "Cindy and I will go grab it from my car."

Eleanor gave us both a small smile and hurried out of the room. Furious, I grabbed Jacques by the arm and started to lead him to the front door. "We need to talk, buddy."

"Ouch, watch your claws!" he yelped. "Those nails of yours could do serious damage to my skin."

The funeral home employee gave us both a funny look as he opened the door. "Thank you for coming," he said quietly.

"We'll be back!" Jacques said, a bit too loudly, as he tried to free himself from my iron grip. "Really, Cin. For someone who recently had a baby, I'd say you have your strength back and then some."

"Anger does strange things to me," I hissed into his ear as we walked carefully toward the car, the parking lot already covered in a thin layer of sleet.

Jacques reached into the back seat for his briefcase. "I already know what you're going to say, darling."

I put my hands on my hips. "How could you go ahead and speak for me like that? You've always let me handle my own transactions in the past." Well, most of the time. There'd been one home I hadn't wanted to list—for personal reasons—but Jacques had encouraged me to do so.

Jacques stared down at the pavement, his face crimson. "I'm sorry about that, love. But desperate times call for desperate measures, and we really need that listing. I promise that I'll do anything you need me to. I'll enter the entire listing on the MLS, arrange everything with the sign man, and take any showings you can't make. Plus, I'll still let you keep your regular share of the commission."

"Jacques, I'm too busy with the baby right now," I protested. "Grace and the rest of my family have to come first."

"But the mother-in-law from hell is helping, right?"

I hesitated. Jacques didn't like to be privy to delicate subjects such as breastfeeding, C-section pain, and other matters. Heck, the incident at the hospital had proven how squeamish he was about childbirth. "There are some activities that I need to be present for."

He flushed with apparent understanding. "Uh, right. Like I said, I'll still give you your full commission and do whatever I can to help. Even though it needs work, that house is worth some serious money."

"Yes, I know it is."

We walked back to the building while I hooked my arm through Jacques' and leaned my head on his shoulder. "Getting tired, darling?" he asked.

"A little," I confessed. "It's the first time I've been out since Grace was born. I guess it's taking me longer to recover this..." I sighed and didn't finish the sentence. "Oh, fine. I'll do it."

Jacques raised his eyebrows at me. "Wow, I didn't even have to bribe you with Starbucks."

I grinned at him sourly. "I have to watch my caffeine intake while I'm—never mind."

"I know that you're worried about the baby," Jacques admitted. "You can do almost everything from home, except actually show the house. There's no need for you to even come into the office unless you want to. I'll have Zoe email all the paperwork to you when it's complete. Maybe I can even add a few more dollars to your commission, as a thank you."

"I'm not doing this for money." We stepped onto the wide-beamed wooden porch that the employee was in the process of salting. He nodded politely to us as we stepped around him and opened the door ourselves this time.

"Come again, dear?" Jacques asked in surprise.

"Yes, I know that sounds hard to believe, especially coming from my mouth," I said wryly. "But it happens to be the truth. Percy asked me to find his killer. Maybe I feel responsible on some level. What if I'd believed what he said about someone setting him up, or if we'd arrived earlier..."

"It wasn't your fault that he died, dear," he said quietly.

I turned to face him. "But I feel responsible on some level. Someone needs to get to the bottom of this. The only people who seemed to have given a damn about him would be Eleanor and maybe Diane. For God's sake, no one even came to the man's funeral." It was too sad and depressing to think about. "Who wanted that house enough to kill him? We need to find out."

Jacques' mouth twisted into a frown. "*We* don't need to do anything. We're simply selling the property and collecting our fair share of a profit. Haven't you been involved in enough murders lately?"

"What about Eleanor? She's staying at the house while she's in town. It technically belongs to her now. What if someone tried to take her out?" I sucked in a breath. "Who would the house go to if something happened to her?"

Jacques pursed his lips. "If something happens to Eleanor, I think it's obvious that the killer's whoever inherits the house from her."

"We've seen some not so obvious killers in the past," I reminded him. "We can talk more about that later. Let's get the contract signed before I change my mind."

He squeezed my hand. "We'll make it work, love."

We started in the direction of the viewing room, when Andrew and his wife walked past us, hand in hand, with their coats on. He gave us a cordial nod while she attempted a half-hearted smile. My guess is that we had been the major topic of their conversation, not Percy.

In the viewing room Eleanor and Diane were sitting next to each other, involved in what looked to be an earnest conversation. They stopped when they caught sight of us.

"I hope we're not interrupting," Jacques said as we approached.

Eleanor and Diane both rose. "Not at all," Eleanor said. "I was telling Diane that you'd agreed to list the house."

Diane smiled politely at us and then addressed Eleanor. "Sure, it's wonderful. But I'm assuming you intend to keep any profit, and you know that will send Tom into another rage." With a sigh she put her coat on. "I'm sorry, but I can't deal with any more of this today." She extended a hand to Jacques and then me. "Thank you both for coming. I know it looks awful that I'm leaving already, but I doubt anyone else will show. Plus, I need to get home to my husband." She lifted an eyebrow at Eleanor. "Before he—he does something stupid." She kissed her on the cheek. "If you need a ride, call me and I'll come back to get you."

Eleanor seemed a bit shell-shocked by Diane's departure but said nothing. After she'd left the room, Eleanor sank back down into her chair and clasped her hands together as if in prayer. "Poor Percy. He didn't deserve this."

Jacques opened his briefcase. "Eleanor, you can sign these later if you want. There's really no rush."

"That's all right." Eleanor took the papers from his outstretched hand. "I'd rather get it all over and done with now. The sooner I can get back to California, the better." She looked thoughtfully at both of us. "Do you happen to know of anyone who would like to help me pack up some items and make a few dollars while doing it? Perhaps you or Jacques have teenaged children who'd be interested?"

"Cindy does." Jacques' face reddened suddenly. "Perhaps you'd want to hire professional packers instead."

Eleanor shook her head. "There are only a few boxes in the attic. It would probably take one afternoon, two at the most."

It was as if she'd given me permission to snoop through Stella's house—an offer I couldn't refuse. If I had the chance to search through Percy and Stella's belongings to find a clue to the killer's identity, it might allow me to prove his innocence. Perhaps Percy's killing was vengeance for Vanessa's death, but something told me there was more to it than that. Whatever the reason, I couldn't let Eleanor know my true intentions. "Well, I have a sixteen-year-old daughter, but she plays volleyball after school most days. I'm sure Jacques and I could give you a couple of hours, though. Right, boss?"

Jacques' eyes almost bugged out of his head. "Cin, I—"

I shot him a warning glance. "We'd probably only be able to do one afternoon. If there's a showing scheduled, all the better. I'll try to arrange it for the same time so we wouldn't have to make multiple trips and disturb you in the process."

Eleanor gave me an appreciative look. "No need to worry about that. I've taken a temporary job at a novelty store while I'm in town. The owner is a friend, and she's always great about letting me make some extra money while I'm in town. Your plan sounds fine to me. I can't pay much, only minimum wage, but it would be such a help. God knows that Stella loved to collect junk. I could understand if the items might fetch some money at an auction, but there's no hope of that. Old books, piles of Tupperware she bought and never used, decks of tarots cards—"

Now she had my full attention. "Tarot cards? She was into them?"

"Oh yes," she said. "Stella got Percy involved as well. The other children were never much interested. Percy used to stay with her during summer vacations, and one year when he was a teenager he became addicted to them. He started going to readings and even drew a card every morning. Stella had a popular phrase that she always said for several years before her death. 'The answer is with the cards.'"

Maybe it wasn't a good idea for me to divulge any information about the crime scene, but it wasn't like the police had sworn me to secrecy either. "I don't know if you're aware of this, but a tarot card was found next to Percy's body."

The smile faded from her lips. "You saw it?"

I shook my head. "Not when I found him. I think Percy might have fallen on top of it. When the police questioned me later, they asked if it was mine. Otherwise I doubt they would have mentioned the card since it's considered part of a crime scene."

Eleanor's face registered disbelief. "This is insane. The first time it happened, I thought it didn't mean anything. Maybe the card had been dropped or was left behind accidentally. Now that it's happened again, there must be some type of significance attached."

She was confusing me. "What are you talking about, *again*?"

Eleanor rested her sober gaze on me. "Why, the tarot cards. When Vanessa died, there was one found next to her body as well."

CHAPTER NINE

"There you have it," Jacques said. "The two murders are related, as you suspected."

"Told you so." I sipped my coffee thoughtfully. We'd stopped at a Starbucks drive-thru for a quick caffeine fix. As much as I longed for a cup of dark-roast coffee, I'd resigned myself to a decaf, while Jacques had his usual nonfat latte.

I'd only been gone for about two hours, but it seemed longer, and I missed Grace already. This was the first time I'd been separated from her since her birth. Had I felt this way after the twins were born? Maybe not. I'd been too much of a zombie during their first year to remember.

Jacques had slowed his usual speed, in part because of the sleet still pouring from the sky but also because he held his drink in one hand. The man was an accident waiting to happen, and I found myself gripping the armrest on the door uneasily. "So, now do you believe me that Percy didn't kill his wife?"

He took a long sip of his beverage and then made a face at me. "You're too nervous."

"I just had a baby, okay? I'd like to get home to her and the rest of my family safely."

Jacques rolled his eyes. "Have I ever let you down, love?"

Okay, he had me on that one. "Why don't you stay for dinner?" I asked as he pulled the vehicle into my driveway. The thought of him eating alone bothered me, and I knew it had become a regular habit for him as of late.

He shook his head. "I'm showing a house to a couple that's only in town for the night. Maybe some other time."

"Then come back after the showing," I insisted.

He rolled his eyes. "Why don't you come right out and ask me? I know that you're dying to."

"Fine. When was the last time you talked to Ed?"

Jacques shrugged. "Three, maybe four days ago. He wanted to know if you got his flowers."

"Yes, they were beautiful. I still need to send him a thank-you card. Come on, Jacques. Tell me what's going on."

He looked away from me and took another sip of his drink. "Nothing is going on—that's the point. I'll be staying at the office until I find another place to live."

"This is crazy!" I burst out. "You're going to destroy your marriage over one little disagreement?"

The look in his eyes stopped me cold. "Cynthia, this isn't some little disagreement. Ed knows how much I've always wanted children. Because of his stubborn streak, we lost out on one child. Who knows if the agency will give us another chance? I can't forgive him for that."

I desperately wanted to knock both of their heads together. Instead, I tried to reason with Jacques. "You can't throw away what you have. It's too precious and rare."

Jacques' jaw quivered for the briefest of seconds, but he stared straight ahead, refusing to look at me. "I don't mean to rush you, love, but my appointment is waiting. What's our next move?"

"Our next move?" I echoed.

"Sure. You plan on doing some snooping around in the attic. What time shall I pick you up?"

He knew me far too well. "Grace usually eats about ten, so maybe around eleven or so. Can I call you and let you know?"

"Yes, my day is pretty flexible." He leaned over and gave me a chaste kiss on the cheek. "Go take care of your precious cargo."

After a moment's hesitation, I opened the car door and eased myself out of the seat. There were still so many things I wanted to say to him. He was going through such a tough time, and all I wanted to do was help. "Hey, Jacques, how about—"

"I'll call you later, darling." He revved the engine, and I took the hint and quickly shut the door before he started to back down the driveway.

I HUMMED SOFTLY to Grace as I laid her back down in the crib then covered her with the quilt that Helen had made for her. Hopefully she wouldn't wake again until at least five o'clock.

The room was quiet and dark, except for a small nightlight burning next to her crib. It was after midnight, and I glanced toward my bed, sorely tempted to return to its cozy warmth. Greg was lying on his side, sound asleep, his arms stretched over my pillow. He looked sexy and relaxed in sleep. For a moment I stood there, listening to him snore softly and thinking about how lucky I was, especially given what Jacques and Ed were currently going through.

Greg had offered to give Grace a supplementary bottle so that I could get some shut-eye when she first started fussing, but I'd told him to go back to bed and then proceeded to nurse her. The poor guy had to leave for work at seven in the morning. My mind was racing in a dozen different directions, and I knew there was no chance of me falling back into a dreamless sleep for a while.

I checked in on the twins and Darcy, who as usual had left her cell phone in bed next to her textbook spread open across her chest. I put both items on her nightstand and turned off the light. Our daughter had matured a lot in the past year, and I was proud of her wanting to succeed and be accepted into a good college. She had aspirations of becoming a teacher someday, which both excited and terrified me. Even though we'd started a college fund for her years ago, there wasn't nearly enough for what she'd need.

I stepped down the stairs quietly, my bare feet creaking on the wood surface. The door to the study was closed, and I missed quiet time at my desk. Helen was snoring loud enough to wake the dead. There must be a set of earplugs around here somewhere.

My laptop was on the kitchen counter where I'd left it earlier. I'd wanted to use it after dinner to do some further research on Percy, but Grace had been fussy and then Stevie had needed help with homework. Seth said he'd done his already, but I suspected that he was lying. I knew he was counting on school being closed tomorrow because of the weather. Greg hadn't arrived home until after seven o'clock himself. He'd ended up putting in a couple of extra hours since he'd taken time earlier in the day to take Grace and me to the doctor.

Glancing out the window, I noticed that the deserted street was covered in a sheet of ice that reflected off the streetlights. The kids would at least have a delay tomorrow, or school might even be closed. That I could handle. What bothered me was the inevitable phone call from the school that would come at approximately four in the morning and undoubtedly wake Grace.

I fixed myself a cup of herbal tea and sat down at the table. I'd phoned Officer Henderson after arriving home from the wake, but he'd been vague and wouldn't reveal any information. I knew from a past murder investigation I'd been involved in that the police were never generous with details. For now, I'd have to see what I could discover on my own.

A vision of Percy's face filled my mind, and once again I heard his voice as he professed his love for Vanessa while he lay dying. I scrunched my eyes shut, but the image was still there. A little research and checking around Eleanor's house couldn't hurt. I figured I owed him that much at least.

I typed Percy's name into Google. Ah, he was popular here and even had his own place on Wikipedia. Several links to articles flooded the Google page concerning Vanessa's death and his recent release from prison. The first articles appeared on September 7, 1996. Vanessa had been murdered the previous day, and Percy had already been taken into custody.

At the time of Vanessa's death, the couple had been married for five years with no children. I found a closeup shot from their wedding that was used in several different articles. Vanessa had been a true beauty, with shoulder-length auburn curls, peaches and cream skin, and picturesque blue eyes. Percy himself had been handsome with dark, wavy hair and a ruddy complexion. He didn't even resemble the man that I had met last week, except in the eyes. In the picture, he stared at his bride with such love and adoration that my heart twitched. How had two people who'd been so happy and in love both ended up brutally murdered?

The wall clock ticked away merrily in my warm and otherwise silent kitchen as I read the numerous articles and stared at various pictures of Percy taken during different stages of his trial—on the steps outside of the courthouse with his lawyer as he pushed a reporter away, a shot of him on the witness stand while he was questioned by the prosecuting attorney, and in the courtroom wearing an orange jumpsuit as he was sentenced—his head down, shoulders slumped forward. Percy had been the only suspect. Witnesses had attested to hearing him threaten Vanessa the day before her death as the couple argued in the center of a busy shopping center parking lot. His exact words to her? "*You'll be sorry for cheating on me, you slut.*"

Cripes. What awful timing. Jacques had mentioned Vanessa's infidelity to me before, and there were a few references to it during the trial. Percy himself had confessed on the stand that Vanessa had been unfaithful but insisted he'd only asked her to stop seeing the other man. He claimed that he never would have hurt his wife.

I could only find one mention about the tarot card left next to Vanessa's body. The source was a Facebook memorial page that had been set up for Vanessa by her sister, Jennifer Benson, over seven years ago. According to the page, she lived in South Carolina. Jennifer commented that Percy had been a "fanatic" about the cards. The one located at the crime scene was more than enough evidence for her that Percy had committed the deed. There were no pictures of the card to be found anywhere, but I figured that there was a chance Jennifer might have seen it. On impulse, I shot off a quick private message to her page.

Hi, Jennifer. You don't know me, but my name is Cindy York. I'm a real estate agent in New York who found Percy Rodgers the other day. There was a tarot card next to his body, and I'm curious if it might match the description of the one found with your sister. I've been asked to help the police with their investigation. Liar, liar, pants on fire. *Please feel free to message me back at your convenience. I look forward to hearing from you.*

She probably wouldn't respond, but hey, it was worth a shot. I closed out Facebook and went on to read another news article about Percy's recent murder. There were over 500 comments attached, and I could not find a single one that sympathized with the man. Although my name hadn't been divulged, there were a couple of references that his last words had been to his real estate agent about the wife he loved so much. The comments by virtual strangers were enough to turn my blood to ice water. Then again, hadn't I thought the exact same thing last week when Jacques first told me that Percy was a convicted killer? It seemed that I was no better than the rest of these people and also as judgmental.

Someone stroked my shoulders from behind, and I nearly jumped in my seat. Greg was standing there in a pair of red plaid boxers and white T-shirt, a concerned look on his face. His hair was tousled, his five o'clock shadow prominent, and he looked incredibly sexy for this early in the morning.

"Holy cow." I placed a hand over my heart. "You scared me to death."

Greg stared down at me and frowned. "It's three o'clock in the morning, baby. What are you doing down here?"

Before I could reply, he glanced over at the laptop screen. The article with its caption, *Rodgers Found Murdered 20 Years After Wife's Killing,* stood out in large bold letters at the top of the screen.

Yes, I was busted.

Greg sighed and ran a hand over his face. "Come on, Cin. Not again."

I clicked out of the article. "I was curious about Percy's wife. That's all."

He fixed his steadfast blue gaze upon me. "That's *not* all. You're planning to play amateur detective and get involved in another murder investigation again."

"That's not it." I shook my head vehemently. "I want to—"

Greg sat down in the chair next to me and reached for my hand. "That's the reason you agreed to take the listing from that woman, Eleanor, isn't it? It's not about the sale or money. I know you, baby. You feel guilty about Percy's death. You think that you failed this guy somehow in his hour of need, and that inner detective of yours won't rest until you find out who killed him."

"Inner detective?" I laughed in utter disbelief. "You give me way too much credit."

"Don't joke about this," Greg pleaded. "You haven't even recovered from your surgery yet, and Grace is nursing every three hours. There's too much on your plate right now, and instead of resting, you're down here doing internet searches."

"I can't sleep. This is really bothering me."

He stroked my hand lightly with his fingers. "What's bothering me is how exhausted you are all the time, and now you've gone ahead and taken on this listing. A listing that involves a very bitter family, from what you've said."

"You don't think I can handle it?" I asked.

He shook his head. "I never said that. I've been married to you for almost twenty years and know that you can handle anything. But I am concerned about your health. Didn't you say Jacques was going to take care of all the details?"

"He's planning to, but Jacques has a lot on his plate too. There's some type of leak in our office that in turn is affecting our leads and sales. Plus, he and Ed have officially separated."

Greg's eyes widened in surprise. "Wow. I'm sorry to hear that. I know you said they were having problems, but I figured they'd work it out eventually."

"Yeah, me too. I'm still hopeful though."

He raised a well-defined eyebrow at me. "You think that Percy didn't kill his wife, don't you?"

"I believe he's innocent, yes."

Greg pressed his lips together. "Maybe someone killed him to even the score?"

"No, I'm pretty certain that there's more to it. From what he said to me the day he died, I think he knew his killer—and the person who killed his wife, if they are both the same individual. Eleanor insists that he's innocent too. Sadly, I think we're the only ones who do. The worst part is that no one even seems to care that the poor man is dead. If you could have been at that wake today..." My voice shook slightly. "No one came, Greg.

Only his siblings and their spouses were present, and it was obvious that they didn't want to be there, either."

He continued to stroke my hand in silence.

"His own brother and sister." A lump formed in my throat. "They both left before the end of the calling hours. Would it have really inconvenienced them to stay for four lousy hours? When Jacques and I took off, Eleanor was the only one left, except for the funeral home employees. It's beyond horrible. The man spent 20 years in prison for a crime he didn't even commit! For God's sake, he had a life. No one seems to care that it's over."

"Sweetheart." Greg's voice was hoarse. "Please don't do this to yourself."

My eyes grew moist, and I blinked back tears. I hated to think about death. Like everyone else, I'd lost my fair share of people I had loved. I'd watched my mother die a slow and horrible death from breast cancer and lost my best friend at the tender age of eighteen. My father had died when I was a baby, so sadly, I had no memories of him. "When my time comes, I hope that people will show up. I don't want that to happen to me."

I hadn't realized that I'd said the words out loud until I looked up and saw Greg's startled expression.

"Whoa." He leaned forward in his chair and put his arms around me. "Where is this all coming from? Are you feeling okay? Is this related to the baby's birth?"

"No." I knew what he was getting at. "It's not postpartum depression. At least I don't think so. But her birth has forced me to think about how precious life really is. You and the kids are my world. If something ever happens to me, I don't want you to be sad or alone. I'd want you to get married again."

Greg pulled me onto his lap. "Okay, I really hate this conversation. And don't be so quick to marry me off again. If something happened to you, I honestly don't think I could go on." He buried his face in my hair. "I love you more than anything."

Tears rolled down my cheeks, and he kissed them away. "That's how I feel about you too."

"Look," Greg said as he wove his fingers through my hair. "If it makes you feel better to do some snooping around the house, I won't stop you. But bring Jacques with you, or call me if he's not available. I don't want you to undertake anything dangerous. Have you forgotten that you and Jacques almost got yourselves killed last summer and that you wound up with a broken leg?"

I shuddered at the memory. I'd just found out that I was pregnant, and that had been my wakeup call to how much I wanted this baby. "I promise to be careful. For some strange reason, I keep thinking that there's a clue in that house to help us discover the killer's real identity. I've also got this weird feeling that Percy's grandmother knew the truth."

Greg placed a lingering kiss on my neck. "If she did, I'd like to think she would have gone to the police." He kissed me gently on the mouth. "Okay, I've had enough of these maudlin conversations about death. I have a lot of living left to do, and so does my beautiful wife. Let's go upstairs and turn in."

"Please do." We both jumped at the sound of Helen's angry voice resonating from behind the study's door. "Some people are trying to sleep around here."

CHAPTER TEN

Much to the kids' chagrin, there was only a two-hour delay from school the next morning. They'd been hoping for the day off, and I'd warned the twins to get their homework finished the night before, but my words had fallen upon deaf ears. Seth begged for help with his, while Stevie couldn't find his boots, and the baby fussed all morning and refused to nap. Helen sang Barbara Streisand songs in an off-key voice while she did the breakfast dishes until I thought I might lose my mind.

"Mother," Darcy yelled down the stairs. "Can't you keep those delinquents quiet? I'm trying to get in a little extra studying for my test today!"

"What's a delinquent?" Seth asked Helen.

"Ask your mother, dear," Helen replied. "She sells houses for them."

I sucked in a breath but said nothing. It was tempting to take Grace with me to Eleanor's, but it was freezing out, and she was better off staying here—even if it was with Helen.

"How's the work coming on your house?" I tried to keep my voice casual.

Helen frowned and shook her head in annoyance. "They're nowhere near done."

"Oh, too bad." This was not good news to hear. If she stayed here much longer, I might be tempted to shoot her.

After the kids finally left for school, I fed Grace and managed to get her settled down in her crib. Already wiped out, I went into the bathroom to take a shower. Greg, bless his heart, had insisted on getting up with Grace at five so I could get a few hours of sleep. He had to be tired as well, but we both knew it would be like this for a while. Still, I wouldn't have traded those quality minutes in his arms last night for anything. We rarely had time alone these days, so that made it even more precious. We'd enjoyed a good laugh about Helen's eavesdropping as well.

I phoned Jacques at eleven, and he said he'd be over in ten minutes to get me. Then I placed a call to Eleanor so that she'd know we were on our way.

"I'm leaving the house now and can't wait," she said. "Diane is expecting me, and I'm already late. Tom isn't around, so it's a good time for me to visit."

"Would he be upset if he knew you were there?" I asked.

She paused for a moment. "Let's say that he wouldn't be pleased. Before you arrived at the wake yesterday, Tom lashed out at me. He thinks that somehow I forced Stella into leaving me the house. Who knows? He might believe that I killed Percy as well."

"That's crazy," I protested.

Eleanor sighed. "I'm used to being the black sheep of the family, so to speak. And technically, I'm not even part of the family, which makes things worse. By the way, the sign man left here a little while ago."

"The listing is up online as well," I said. "Jacques took care of that."

"Excellent. I left some storage boxes in the attic. There's a ton of old books and clothes of Eleanor's and Percy's as well. I don't think he unpacked everything after he moved in. Please know how much I appreciate you doing this. Oh, and I also wanted you to know that I'm planning to fly back to California at the end of the week."

"So soon?" I asked, surprised.

"Is that a problem? I've signed the papers, and Percy's being cremated today. I don't believe I'm needed for any other reason, and to be honest, I don't want to be here any longer."

"No. We can do everything long distance, even the closing documents." Eleanor's voice sounded anxious and made me curious. "Are you afraid of something?"

"I don't know." Her voice trembled on the other end of the line. "I guess I'm worried, after what happened to Percy. What if the killer wants something in this house and won't stop until they find it?"

If someone was harboring ill will about Eleanor inheriting the house, it was possible her life could be in danger. Personally, I thought there might be more to it. I was certain that Percy's murder connected to Vanessa's somehow.

Percy had implied that he knew who'd set him up. Maybe he had confronted the person right before he died and that in turn led to his murder. As much as I wanted to snoop around the house, I had to be honest with her. "Perhaps you should be the one to look through all the items in the attic. There may be something that offers a clue as to who did this."

"Well, I don't know what it would be," she declared. "There's nothing but junk. And to answer your question, no, I don't want to search up there myself. I have a horrible allergy to dust and wouldn't care to try to undertake it. Nothing good will come from this, that's for sure."

Did Eleanor know more than she was letting on? "Is the family aware that you're leaving?" Maybe it would be better if she didn't tell them anything.

"Diane knows," she said. "I'm sure she's told Tom as well."

Great. "How would you feel about doing an open house this weekend? We're sure to have people stopping by."

"The sooner I can get out of here the better," she said. "An open house is fine. You're the boss now."

I decided to take the plunge. "You said that Stella was convinced Percy didn't kill Vanessa. Is it possible she has proof?"

"Proof of his innocence, you mean?"

"Yes. Otherwise, how could she be so sure? Do you think Stella knew who Vanessa's killer was?"

There was a long silence on the other end. When Eleanor spoke again, her voice was low and full of emotion. "Yes, I think that she might have, but she never breathed a word about it to me. I understand what you're getting at. Maybe there is something hidden in the house. With her illness it's possible she could have put a clue aside and then forgotten where it was later. Still, it's too much to fathom how she'd let her own grandson rot in jail if she'd known the truth." She paused. "Diane's outside. I have to go." She clicked off without another word.

When I looked out the kitchen window again, I spotted Jacques pulling into my driveway. Helen was watching *The Price is Right* in the study, and I went to the doorway to say good-bye. "I've pumped a couple of bottles for Grace, but you may not need them. I shouldn't be more than two or three hours."

She waved a hand absently in the air and didn't even look at me. "Have a good time with your fruity friend."

Heat rose through my face. "Please don't disrespect Jacques like that, Helen."

She ignored me and continued to stare at the screen, where an elderly lady was jumping up and down and hugging Drew Carey next to the big wheel. I started to walk away then thought better of it. I was not going to let this go anymore. "Helen, if you'd like to go home, I can always call a babysitter."

She turned around and pinned me with an icy blue gaze.

"Home to what? I have no roof, remember? Would you like me to freeze to death? Or perhaps have something fall on my head while I'm asleep at night?"

My mouth quivered at the corners. *Stop thinking such naughty thoughts, Cindy.* "Maybe you'd prefer I don't answer that, Helen." Then I hurried out the kitchen door before saying something else I'd regret later.

"Uh-oh," Jacques said when he saw my face. "Mother-in-law of the year must be at it again. Let me guess—she made a dig at me this time."

He must have some sort of psychic powers. "How did you know?"

"Give me a little credit, darling," he said as we pulled out of the driveway. "I know what she thinks of me. That woman has enough venom in her to make a snake jealous."

Conversations about my mother-in-law always made me ill, so I changed the subject. "Eleanor's flying home in a couple of days. She doesn't want to be here any longer."

"Well, I can't say that I blame her," Jacques admitted. "She's already signed the papers, so there's no reason for her to stay. By the way, I got a call from an interested party a little while ago. They want to see the house later this afternoon, and I told them it wasn't a problem."

I groaned. "Jacques, I can't be away from the baby for too long. Oh, and I totally forgot to ask Eleanor, but I'm assuming the crime scene has been cleaned up?"

He nodded and stared straight ahead. "It was cleaned up days ago, but she had a service in this morning, per my suggestion. As you know, we don't have to divulge that he died in the house, but I'm guessing that everyone is already aware. Maybe we'll get lucky and find an out-of-town buyer."

"That would be nice." I tried not to let the doubt in my voice show. "Are we selling the house as is? I can't see Eleanor sinking any money into it."

He turned into the driveway. "If we don't get any nibbles after the first month, we'll talk to Eleanor about reducing the number, but I feel it's fairly priced." He placed the car in park. "The latest rumor going around in the newspapers is that Percy did himself in, which you and I both know is unlikely. People love buying into that theory. They want to believe it was a suicide—that Percy so regretted killing his wife that he had tortured himself all these years and then decided to end it all. I guess it makes him sound more humane to them."

"That's insane," I said. "He didn't kill Vanessa. I wish I could shout it to the world."

"But they won't listen to you," Jacques protested. "In everyone's eyes, he's a cold-blooded killer. On top of everything, we now have to spend an afternoon going through all that crap in the attic. Do you think we'll find anything to help prove Percy's innocence?"

We stepped onto the front porch, which creaked underneath us in welcome. "Eleanor said that there are only books and clothes up there. Still, it couldn't hurt, right?"

"Well, only this once," he grumbled. "Sales may be down, but even so, I don't have time to dig through someone else's garbage."

"You and Ed need to make up soon," I said as we climbed the winding staircase to the fourth floor. I had to pause a couple of times to catch my breath. "You're turning into a regular fussbudget. Plus, what's with the suit? There's probably a pile of dust in that room an inch thick. You should have dressed down —in jeans and a T-shirt."

He cocked an eyebrow at me in disbelief. "Have you ever seen me in jeans? I've worn suits for so long that the word denim doesn't exist in my vocabulary anymore. By the way, you're looking pale, darling. You should have asked Darcy to come instead. Are you in any condition to be climbing stairs yet?"

I waved a hand in dismissal. "I have stairs in my house too."

"You had a baby last week," Jacques said as we reached the attic. "Frankly, racing you to the hospital once is more than enough for me in an entire lifetime."

"There's that sarcasm shining through," I teased. "The real Jacques I know and love."

The room was large and chilly, due to a lack of insulation in the walls. The wooden floor, like the rest of the house, was scratched and worn, and solid oak beams were sticking out from the raised ceiling above. There were six cedar trunks and various cardboard boxes filled with clothing that looked like it had belonged to Stella. Other boxes held books that ranged from a wide selection of Little Golden Books children's stories to hardback copies of Moby Dick and Harry Potter novels. "Looks like Stella was quite the reader." I opened the cover to a copy of James Joyce's *Ulysses*. "Oh, wait a second. Percy's name is written in here."

Jacques took off his navy suit coat and matching tie then rolled up his sleeves, ready for action. "Do you know what Percy's occupation was before he went to prison?"

I grabbed an empty cardboard box from the stack and started to place the books inside. "I read in one of the articles online that he was a newspaper reporter."

"Newspaper reporters don't make a great deal of money," Jacques said. "Well, not ones for smaller presses at least. It seems that didn't matter though. According to the articles I've read, Percy and Vanessa lived here for a while, and then Stella put them up in their own house. After Vanessa was killed and Percy went to jail, Diane and Tom moved into their home. They still live there."

This startled me. "Really? How weird. Do you think Stella allowed them to move in, or did they take possession on their own?"

"With Tom, it wouldn't surprise me if he just moved right in,"

Jacques muttered as he folded several pieces of Stella's wardrobe that looked like they had been designed with Woodstock in mind. There were love beads, flowing skirts, and flare-legged jeans. "I checked out Diane and Tom's house on the MLS last night. The house was still in Stella's name when she died six months ago. I'm assuming it must have gone to them in the will, unless there's another mysterious document that declares Eleanor owns it as well."

I shuddered inwardly. Eleanor wasn't exactly popular with most of the Rodgers family members these days, and this would not help.

"Did you ever see so many books?" Jacques complained as he stopped to examine a well-worn copy of *Paradise Lost*. "We might need more boxes at this rate."

"Percy being a writer might explain all the books." I placed a copy of *To Kill a Mockingbird* in another box. I couldn't believe that Eleanor didn't want any of these treasures. Some of these books looked like first editions and had to be worth money. Eleanor had insisted that they be shipped off to a local second-hand bookstore that she was fond of.

"Look at this," Jacques held up a packet of cards. "More tarot cards. Maybe we should consult someone about the cards left at the crime scene and see what they mean. I happen to know an excellent psychic."

I told him how I'd reached out to Vanessa's sister but hadn't heard back yet. "We could go ahead and schedule a time to meet with your…ah…friend. But we'll need information about the card found with Vanessa's body first."

"How about tomorrow?" Jacques suggested. "Even if you haven't heard back yet, we could still plan on it. At least Yvette might be able to shed some light on the one found with Percy. If the killer is sending us a message, she might be able to tell us what it is."

"I've never been to a psychic before." It sounded a bit terrifying, but I didn't want to tell Jacques about my unfounded fears. Instead, I lifted another pile of books and noticed one with a plaid cloth cover. On closer inspection, I realized it was a diary. "Hey, check this out. I think I found Percy's diary."

Jacques came up behind me and peered over my shoulder. "This could be a great help, Cin. Maybe he wrote down thoughts about Vanessa's death."

I thumbed through the pages, which had started to turn yellow, and the realization hit me. "These entries might be from before he went to prison." Excitement stirred within me at the possibility. Entries were sparse with no dates attached, and I thumbed through to the end and then read the second to last one aloud. The cursive writing was cramped and difficult to make out.

"Funny, it doesn't look like his writing," I mused. "Listen to this. 'It's so dull here. The only time I have any fun is when we're together. I can't wait for our next time.' Oh wow. Maybe this belonged to Stella? Do you think she was referring to a lover?"

Jacques flipped the page. "Here's the last entry. I can't make it out."

I squinted at the writing for a minute. "Okay, I think I've got it. 'This is too much to take. I can't continue with this charade anymore.'" The hairs started to rise on the back of my neck. "'He said he'll kill me if I leave. The scary part is that I know he'll do it.'"

"Yikes," Jacques said. "Someone wanted to kill Stella as well? What's with this family?"

I flipped the book over and looked inside the front cover. The letters *VR* were printed in large black letters.

"Oh God," I breathed. "This isn't Stella's diary. It's Vanessa's."

CHAPTER ELEVEN

Shortly after finding the diary, Jacques and I decided to wrap things up for the day. He promised to come back for the showing scheduled later in the day, which left me free to get home to the baby and the rest of my family. We'd already been here for over two hours, and I was tired and sore and needed to call it quits. Greg was right. I had to be careful about my health and overdoing it. The last thing I wanted was to wind up back in the hospital.

I'd thought about leaving the diary behind to show Eleanor but at the last minute decided to take it with me. I planned to reread it later on to make sure I hadn't missed anything important. At some point I should turn it over to the police, but for now I was hesitant. As far as I was concerned, it would only incriminate Percy further in the murder of his wife. Still, I didn't believe he was guilty and wanted to help clear his name.

Upon arriving home, I found the twins downstairs watching television, while Darcy had stayed after school for volleyball practice. Helen was sweeping the kitchen floor.

She put a finger to her lips. "Grace is asleep." Her voice

sounded almost victorious. "She fell right asleep in my arms and didn't miss you one bit."

This was another one of those moments when I felt like smacking the woman upside the head. Instead of growing more tolerant of her every day, it was the opposite. I wanted Helen out of my house. Greg and I would need to have a serious talk tonight when we went to bed. If we could manage to stay awake long enough for one, that is.

Helen got by on a decent pension from her former employment with the State of New York and a life insurance policy that Greg's father had left her. She could hole up in a hotel for a few days, and I'd manage to take care of my children without her assistance. After almost 19 years of this woman's sly digs and sarcastic remarks, I'd finally had all I could stand.

As I climbed the stairs to check on Grace, my phone pinged from my pants pocket. I drew it out and saw that I had a Facebook instant message. My heart gave a little jolt when I noticed who it was from. Jennifer Benson, Vanessa's sister.

Hello, Cindy. Thanks for reaching out. I'm sorry you had to be the one to find that bastard's body. I only hope that he suffered as much as my sister did.

Yikes. Even though I had suspected she would react this way, her words still sent a chill through me. I read on.

As for the tarot card that was found next to Vanessa, I don't remember much about its meaning. Something to do with swords, I believe. I've attached a picture that the prosecutor showed at Percy's trial. The attorney said it was from one of Percy's decks. In a pathetic attempt to defend himself, Percy said people who really believed in tarot would never have used the cards in such a manner. He kept insisting that he was framed.

Any excitement I experienced over this statement quickly died when I read the next sentence.

But I know the truth and hope he rots in hell.

God bless, Jennifer.

There wasn't much I could say in response to that. Jennifer would probably become angry if I insisted Percy was innocent. I shot off a quick message and thanked her profusely for her time. There was no point in engaging in further conversation with her—at least not now. I pressed Jacques' number on speed dial and waited in the hallway, not wanting to wake Grace with our conversation.

Jacques picked up after the first ring. "What can I do for you, love?"

"Did you manage to get a hold of your friend Yvette, the fortune teller?"

"Ahem." He cleared his throat. "Get it right—she is a psychic. And yes, she did text me back and said she has some free time tomorrow afternoon. I was all set to go her office, but she offered to come out to Eleanor's. Something about it helping with her aura."

The whole psychic thing was not winning me over, but I decided not to say so. "I thought she was only a reader?"

"Oh no. She dabbles in a little bit of everything," Jacques said dryly. "Kind of like a painter."

An interesting comparison. "I heard back from Vanessa's sister, and she sent me a picture of the other tarot card. We can ask Yvette about both of them now."

"Excellent. I'm back at Eleanor's. The showing agent didn't have my number, so she called the office, and Zoe phoned to tell me that they're running about 15 minutes late. They were looking at another house. Not a good sign, if you ask me. Maybe they were so interested in the other place that they didn't want to leave it." He sounded depressed.

In some ways, it was as if Jacques and I had changed roles. He had never been one to act so insecure—that was my job. Jacques was always so confident and self-assured, and this sudden lack of self-esteem bothered me. "It's going to get better. With spring on the way, sales are bound to pick up. Remember that seminar we went to last month? They said things would turn around soon and it would be a stellar seller's market this year."

"It better be," Jacques said grimly. "Oh, and more good news. When I got back to the office this afternoon, Arielle Jones handed me her resignation. She said she can't make enough money here, so she's joining another agency. She wasn't gone two minutes when Stacey came running up to me and asked if she could have her office."

"That seems a bit tacky." Stacey Loudon was a new agent at Forte Realty, having joined us last fall. She was young, perky, and after everyone else's business. I'd dealt with her kind before, and this didn't concern me since I knew Jacques had my back. A sudden thought niggled at my brain. "You don't think Arielle left because *she* was giving out leads, do you?"

His reply came without hesitation. "No, I don't. I've known Arielle for years and trust her as much as I do you. But going forward, let me say that I will be keeping a closer eye on Stacey."

"Sounds like a wise decision," I agreed.

"Oh, a car just drove up, love. I'll text later and let you know how the showing went."

I clicked off and quietly opened the door to my bedroom. Grace was sleeping in her crib like a little angel. Since the twins weren't due home for another hour and I had no desire to spend quality time with Helen downstairs, I decided to take a quick snooze myself. As soon as my head hit the pillow, I was in dreamland.

A loud noise punctuated my eardrum. Someone was eating in my dream—*no*, someone was eating in my bed. I opened my eyes slowly to see Stevie sitting next to me, munching away on crackers. Rusty was busy licking up the crumbs off the comforter.

"Hi, Mom," Stevie said, and he continued to crunch away.

I sat up and rubbed my eyes. "You know you're not supposed

to eat in here." I glanced over at the crib and noticed that the baby wasn't there. "Does Grandma have Grace?"

"No, she went home for a while. Grandma said you were up here with the baby, so we grabbed snacks and came to hang out with you."

I jumped off the bed and ran to the crib, looked inside it again and then underneath. Desperately I tried to stay calm. "Where's your sister?"

Stevie popped another cracker into his mouth. "Seth has her in our room. He said he'll take care of her. He's a great babysitter, Mom. She's not even crying anymore. I think he changed her diaper too. Want a cracker?"

Dear God. How long had I been asleep? I ran across the hall in a panic. Seth was lying on his bed, reading a Captain Underpants book. Grace was down at the foot of the bed, teetering dangerously near the edge. Her onesie was unbuttoned, and the diaper was half on, half off.

"Hi, Mom," Seth said proudly. "I changed the baby all by myself."

I snatched her up in my arms and allowed myself to breathe again. Grace's eyes were wide open and darting around the room, almost as if she wondered what was in store for her next. I cradled her close to my chest and tried to get my bearings together. I'd never dreamed that the boys would try to pick her up or change her diaper for that matter. They'd both held Grace in the hospital and hadn't seemed that interested in her.

"Seth," I whispered through clenched teeth. "You are *never* to do that again. Grace almost fell off the bed. A fall like that could have hurt her badly!"

The smile left Seth's face, and his lower lip quivered. "I'm sorry."

Stevie's voice piped up from behind me, in defense of his brother. "We wanted to see what was so great about her. You spend all your time with her now. It's like we're not even here."

Seth turned away and flopped over onto his stomach. "Shut up, dummy. Like I even care."

My heart tore in two as I watched the twins' reactions. I should have been prepared for this. Greg and I'd had the new baby talk with them months ago, but the boys had seemed fine back then. Perhaps since they had each other, I didn't think they would be as affected by Grace's arrival. Boy, had I been wrong.

I sat down on the edge of Seth's bed with Grace in my arms and rubbed a hand over his hair. "I'm sorry, guys. Grace is a new baby, and she's going to need a great deal of my attention for a while, until she can do some things on her own. But that doesn't mean I love you any less. I want you to hold your sister—hug her and help take care of her—but when I'm here to help too. Okay?"

"Okay," Stevie agreed.

"Now, I need you both to promise me that you won't take Grace out of her crib again without asking me first." I tried to keep my voice steady, but it shook slightly when I thought of what could have happened. "Babies can get hurt very easily."

Seth turned over in the bed and looked at me. "Can we help feed her?"

"Sure, you can give her a bottle sometimes. There are other things you can do to help too—like burp Grace or help fold her clothes."

"I guess that would be okay." Stevie looked at his brother for confirmation.

Seth frowned and pursed his lips together. "I don't think I ever want a baby. They're too much work." He stared at me with sudden suspicion. "How'd you take care of both of us, if one baby's a lot of work?"

"Your father helped a lot." God bless him. Back then, we were both so sleep deprived that we'd walked around in a semiconscious state most of the time. Whenever the twins looked at family photo albums, they'd complained there weren't many pictures of them as babies. We'd been too exhausted to take any.

"Grandma said that you're too old to have a baby," Stevie volunteered.

I called her a nasty name in my head. "Oh, really."

"Yep." Seth bobbed his head back and forth. "She said something about how you should get your tub tied so you don't wind up with your own baseball team. Whatever that means."

Stevie furrowed his brow. "What's a bathtub have to do with more babies? I don't understand."

I clenched my teeth together in annoyance. Helen needed to relocate to the other side of the earth. Then again, it still wouldn't be far enough away. "Your grandmother says a lot of things that I don't understand."

"I like baseball," Stevie remarked. "Can we try out for little league this year?"

"Sure, you can. Now, why don't I put Grace back in her crib, and we'll go downstairs for a snack. Anything you guys want."

Seth jumped off the bed excitedly. "Can we have ice cream sundaes?"

The temperature outside was only ten degrees, but ice cream knew no boundaries. "Why not? I could use one too."

"Hey, Mom?" Stevie asked. "How old is Dad?"

"Forty-six."

A frown creased his face. "Are you sure?"

"Positive," I laughed. "Why?"

Stevie looked confused. "But Grandma said she's only forty-nine."

CHAPTER TWELVE

"Hey." Jacques shook my arm slightly. "Wake up. We're here, love."

Confused, I rubbed my eyes and tried to remember where *here* was. I'd met Jacques at the office so that I could check the leads list and my mail. The list had proven to be dismal once again, so we'd quickly departed and driven over to Eleanor's, where we were to meet Yvette. Although it was only a fifteen-minute drive from the office, that hadn't stopped me from taking a little snooze in Jacques' car.

"Wow." I blinked and sat up in my seat. "I can't believe that I fell asleep." Grace had woken up three times last night, and the sleep deprivation that went along with being a new mother had already caught up to me. "I can't wait to start having my full-caffeinated dosages of Starbucks again."

Jacques' piercing green eyes stared at me with concern. "Darling, may I be honest?"

I yawned. "Aren't you always?"

"You look like death warmed over. This is too much for you. I told you that I'd handle everything with the listing, including the showings."

"Maybe you're right. But I did want to meet the reader in person." I released my seat belt then looked in my side mirror in time to see a red BMW pull up behind us. The vanity license plate said *TREADER*. "Is that Yvette? What's with the plate? Is she a swimmer too?"

Jacques rolled his eyes. "It stands for tarot reader, of course. You've a lot to learn, my dear."

Apparently so. "Seriously, what do you know about this woman? Maybe she's a hoax."

He reached into the back seat for his briefcase. "Okay, do me a favor. Lose that cynical look on your face. It's shining through and not like a ray of sunshine. For the record, no, I don't think she's a fake. Besides, what would it matter? We only want to know what the cards mean. There's no charge involved, so what do we have to lose?"

"Why is she doing this for free?" I tried to keep the skepticism out of my voice.

Jacques proudly stuck his nose out in the air. "If you must know, I did offer to pay for her time today, but she refused. I sold Yvette's house last year and even managed to get her ten grand above the asking price." He gave me a superior grin. "There aren't many people who can do that."

He was right. It was one thing for me to obtain a listing but quite another for me to end up selling it. And above the asking price? That was a pipe dream—like my mother-in-law and me tolerating each other one day.

We got out of the car, and a moment later Yvette joined us on the front porch. Jacques reached out a hand to her.

"Hello, Jacques. Lovely to see you as always." She gave him a peck on the cheek, and then her inquisitive dark eyes settled on me. "Is this Cynthia?"

Hmm. Shouldn't she know this already? She's supposed to be a psychic, after all. "Nice to meet you."

Yvette appeared to be about my age, with black hair

perfectly styled into a French twist and teeth so white that she looked like she'd recently stepped out of a Colgate commercial. She was dressed in an expensive-looking brown trench coat and leather boots to match. Her sunglasses and purse both bore the distinct mark of Gucci, and she had a diamond ring on her left hand about the size of a walnut. If Yvette was a fake, she was obviously very good at it.

Yvette surveyed me with interest. "I know what you're thinking," she said. "If I were really a psychic, wouldn't I have known your name already?"

"Oh no," I lied and stared at the ground, undoubtedly giving myself away. "I didn't think that at all."

She laughed. "I'm only teasing you. No worries, I wasn't trying to read your mind. Everyone always thinks the same thing during introductions, believe me." She continued to observe my face closely. "How interesting that you would like a reading done to help assist you with a murder investigation, darling." Her accent was thick, and the last word rolled off her tongue, making her sound like she was doing a Zsa Zsa Gabor imitation.

"Oh no," I said again, finding myself more than a bit paranoid. She was probably not impressed with my limited vocabulary. "No reading is necessary. We only want to know what different tarot cards mean."

Jacques had already unlocked the house and held the door open wide so that we could both enter. Yvette removed her glasses and stared around at her surroundings. Her smile immediately turned upside down. "Oh my," she breathed. "Such sadness abounds in this house."

Uneasiness washed over me. "As Jacques probably told you, Percy Rodgers was killed here last week."

She nodded but said nothing as she followed us into the great room at a slow pace, taking time to touch the walls and place her hands on the frame of an oil painting of Stella that hung above the fireplace. "I am aware of the stabbing. Everyone in the area knows about it. The sadness that I speak of has been here for a very long time, though. Either someone else was sick or died here. Perhaps Percy's wife?"

Jacques shook his head. "Her murder happened in the home that she shared with Percy."

Yvette's full lips twisted into a frown. "I see. Well, perhaps the illness then."

"Yes," Jacques put in. "The original owner suffered from dementia for years."

Yvette placed a hand on the fireplace mantle and then looked over at both of us. "Why don't you believe, Cindy?"

"What I believe isn't important," I said in all honesty. "Our sole purpose is to find out what the cards mean. We're hoping they might offer a clue to the killer's identity."

Yvette sat down behind Percy's desk, and her eyes did a full scan of the room. She pursed her lips together and then stared down at the floor. "This is where it happened. Mr. Rodgers died in this room, didn't he? At this desk, perhaps?"

I swallowed nervously and nodded. There was no way she could have known that, at least I didn't think so. The articles in the newspaper stated that Percy had died at home, but there were scant details provided.

Jacques wiped his glasses with a handkerchief and then returned them to his face. "Yvette, I can't remember if I told you this on the phone, but the house originally belonged to Percy's grandmother. Now that he's deceased, the house has passed on to a good friend of Stella's—a woman by the name of Eleanor Cassidy."

I placed the deck of tarot cards we'd found upstairs in front of Yvette. "Percy was very interested in tarot. We were told that he drew a card every day."

Yvette lifted the deck between her blood red acrylic nails and examined it. "The correct term is that he did a spread every day. My goodness, this is an old one." She glanced through a few of the cards and frowned. "There appears to be some missing from the deck. What did the card look like that was found next to Percy's body?"

"I don't have it on me." How I wished I'd taken a picture of it when Officer Henderson had shown it to me in the hospital, but that probably would have sent up a red flag to the man. "I remember it well. There was a picture of a man without shoes, and he was wearing ragged clothes. He had on a floral shirt and carried a stick on his back."

"Feathers," Jacques interrupted. "He had feathers in his hand, too."

"Ah yes." Yvette pursed her lips. "That is known as the fool card."

Jacques snapped his fingers. "So the killer was making fun of Percy. Maybe because Percy went to jail for a crime that he didn't commit?"

"That must be the message the killer was trying to convey," I said excitedly. "The killer must have known tarot as well. Maybe he or she even practiced it with Percy." I nudged Jacques in the ribs. "Eleanor might have an idea as to who it was."

Yvette held up a hand. "Whoa, my dears. You are getting far ahead of yourselves. In the first place, a true believer in tarot would not use the cards in such a manner."

"What do you mean?" I thought of Percy's admission in court.

"Most people know the significance of the fool card, or at least they think that they do," Yvette explained. "The fool, also known as the vagabond, may be used to symbolize one's walking through life, as in a fool's game. There are many different meanings that can be interpreted from the card. It also depends if the card was reversed or not."

"Reversed?" I asked, puzzled.

"If the card was upside down when it was found, it is considered reversed. Then there would be other meanings associated with it," Yvette said.

Cripes. "This is more complicated than I thought."

She laughed. "People think that they can google a card and find out all they need to know, but there's so much more to it. Tarot structures our spiritual knowledge. It is not just meant to tell one's fortune."

"This means that the killer may not have been versed in tarot at all," I put in.

Yvette nodded. "Correct. Percy's wife was killed approximately twenty years before him, I believe? Do you know if he was interested in tarot back then?"

"Yes, ever since he was a teenager," I replied.

"Then it's possible that this person—the killer or *killers*—knew of his interest, and that's how they chose to frame him for the murder." Yvette shut her eyes for a second. "It must have been someone who knew Mr. Rodgers fairly well."

"Maybe a family member or a friend," Jacques put in.

His words sent a shiver down my spine, and I wrapped my arms around my middle. There was a good possibility that I may have already met Percy's killer, and the thought did not fill me with joy.

Yvette leaned back in the chair. "Do you have a picture of what the card left next to Percy's wife looked like?"

I dug my phone out of my purse and brought up the message from Jennifer. "Vanessa—err, the woman who was killed—her sister sent me a picture of the card through Facebook. I have no idea what it might mean though. The only thing that stood out for me was the swords."

Yvette studied the card with intense concentration. "Ah yes. This is the Two of Swords. See how the woman is blindfolded and holds a sword in each hand? She sits before a sea filled with rocks and crags that present obstacles to ships that need to have clear passage. If the card was intended for Vanessa, the person who left it may have been trying to show she was confused about her situation, like the woman in the card who wears the blindfold. Perhaps that she can see neither the problem nor the solution clearly. Now, if the card was upright when found, it might mean she was indecisive, with blocked emotions. For this particular card the meanings are very similar for both upright and reverse positions." She pursed her lips. "It sounds as if Vanessa did not know what she should do about something."

The diary entry that I'd read yesterday came to mind. "Vanessa was confused. I also think she knew her life was in danger."

Yvette raised a pencil thin eyebrow at me. "How do you know that?"

I hesitated. Jacques trusted Yvette explicitly, and a part of me wanted to as well, but if I revealed what I knew so far, it made Percy sound guilty, and something deep down inside me refused to believe it. Not wanting to delve into this further, I chose to change the subject. "So, this card could symbolize a woman who was torn between two men. A woman who was cheating on her husband."

"It's possible," Yvette conceded. "But it could mean something else too. Perhaps she had to make a choice and could not decide. What path or man to follow, so to speak." She brought my phone closer to her face. "Was this card ripped when it was found?"

I took the phone from her hands and squinted down at it. Sure enough, it was torn almost halfway through. "I guess I didn't look that closely before." Some detective I was. "Do you think that's symbolic as well?"

"That's difficult to say. There are so many different meanings to interpret." She scooped up the deck of cards in her hands and gestured for me to sit on the other side of the desk. "I have a very strong feeling about your aura. Let's do a reading. Would you like Jacques to leave the room so we have complete privacy?"

"No, he doesn't have to leave." I shot Jacques a look, which was more like a plea for help, but he either didn't catch on or chose to ignore it instead.

Jacques green eyes shone like a cat's. "This is going to be fun."

My mouth went dry. "Yvette, a reading isn't necessary. You've been very helpful, but I only want to—"

Yvette narrowed her eyes. "Please sit down, Cindy."

Once again, I glanced at Jacques, who mouthed the word *sit* to me. Like a dog, I obeyed and flopped back in the chair. *How do I get myself into these things?*

Yvette handed me the deck. "Go ahead and shuffle the cards."

I obeyed, clumsily moving the cards back and forth between my hands. I was a terrible card player and an equally awful shuffler. To her credit, Yvette waited patiently, her eyes focused upon me the entire time, which only made me feel more awkward. I held out the deck to her, and she placed three cards each into three separate groups down in front of me—one to the far left of the desk, another in the center, and the last set on the right. Yvette pointed to the group on my left.

"These cards represent your past," she said. "Sorrow and joy. Some danger." She went on to the next section. "These are your present." She pointed at one card and smiled. "There is a great deal of love in your life." She looked at the next one and frowned. "But you are also conflicted about something."

"Well, I would like to know who did this to Percy," I admitted.

Yvette continued to watch me with those expressive dark eyes of hers. "This is *your* reading. Perhaps it does not have to do with the murder at all. The card may mean that you are confused about something in your personal life."

She was starting to annoy me—maybe because she was spot-on with her assumption. I tried to laugh it off. "Confused about what?"

"You tell me," Yvette smiled. "Perhaps your marriage or job."

My face grew warm. "I'm not confused about anything. I have a wonderful husband and four beautiful children. My family life is perfectly fine, thank you very much."

Her mouth turned upwards at the corners, as if I'd amused her. "There is no need for you to be defensive, Cindy. This may have nothing to do with your family. Perhaps it concerns your career." She ran a slim finger down the side of the card. "Maybe you still have doubts about taking this listing. Or you are thinking about moving away from real estate altogether."

I glanced nervously up at Jacques, who was still standing behind Yvette. When our gazes met, he raised an eyebrow in question. Embarrassed, I looked away. There *was* something on my mind, but I was not about to confess it to a complete stranger. Desperate for a diversion, I pointed to the group of cards on my right. "I assume these are my future?"

Yvette looked at the cards as if seeing them for the first time. Then she pursed her lips together and nodded gravely. "Yes, they are."

"More confusion?" I asked in a somewhat taunting manner. "Gee, what should I have for breakfast tomorrow?"

"Cindy," Jacques growled at me, his voice taking on a warning tone.

"These cards do not specify confusion," Yvette said. "They are about something else."

My stomach convulsed as I stared at the cards. I had no idea what they might mean. "What do they mean, then?"

She pointed at one. "This symbolizes danger. You and a person you love will be in a very bad situation soon." Yvette swallowed hard then brought her solemn gaze level with mine. "I believe that someone will die."

CHAPTER THIRTEEN

"What a crock," I laughed as we watched Yvette's car turn off the street in front of us. "Well, at least it wasn't a total loss. We did find out about the cards and what they might mean."

A muscle ticked in Jacques' jaw, but he said nothing as I continued to plod on. "No wonder she drives a BMW. There must be a ton of people who believe that garbage. What's her hourly rate—two hundred? Hey, it goes to show—"

"Please stop," Jacques said sharply as he pulled his convertible over to the side of the road.

Puzzled, I looked around. "What are you doing? Is something wrong with the car?"

Jacques' brilliant eyes glittered in the sunlight as they bore into mine. "No, Cynthia Ann. Something is wrong with *you*."

I clenched my teeth together. "And what's *that* supposed to mean?"

"You're making a complete fool out of yourself," Jacques went on. "First off, Yvette was nice enough to come out to the house for nothing. Free, zero money involved, zilch. Plus, if she's such a BS artist, how did she know the things that she knew? She was obviously aware that you'd been in danger before. She knew that Percy had been killed in that same room. Explain that."

I couldn't and honestly didn't want to. "Maybe Yvette knows someone on the police force who's been feeding her information."

Jacques rolled his eyes at me and put the car in drive again. "You are unbelievable. Darling, you know there's something to what she said, but you don't want to admit it. Please be careful. Remember what she said—about the bad situation."

"She's putting a death wish on my head," I grumbled. "If Yvette is so attuned to everything, how come she doesn't know who the killer is, then?"

"The tarot cards don't operate that way." Jacques took a left into the paved parking lot adjacent to his office building. "She already told you. The cards don't specify if a particular event will happen. They are used more as a prescient to caution. For example, someone may or may not harm you."

I eyed him with sudden suspicion. "You seem to know a lot about tarot."

He shrugged. "I've had a couple of readings in the past. They were pretty spot-on, so yes, I'm a believer."

Defeated, I sighed. "This is hard for me to accept. My mother was always against anything that had to do with the psychic world. Once, when I was a teenager, I went to a fortune-teller with friends. It was only for fun, but when Mom found out, she was furious and grounded me for two weeks."

"Perhaps she was afraid of the unknown." Jacques paused for a moment, letting silence permeate the vehicle. "Like you."

I stared out the window and didn't answer. There was no need. Jacques already knew that he had me. Yes, I did have a fear of the unknown. It was the same sensation I'd experienced when friends of mine forced me to play the Ouija board with them at a birthday party when I was a teenager. To this day, I was positive I had seen my father's ghost in the room.

We both got out of the car, and I glanced around. The parking lot was empty, except for my vehicle. Zoe must have taken off early.

Jacques fumbled with his key ring at the door. "Now about the open house tomorrow—"

"Whoa. Wait a second. I thought it was on Sunday?"

Jacques shook his head. "I told you last night that I scheduled the ad in the newspaper for tomorrow. There's already a ton for Sunday, so I thought maybe we'd have a better shot if we held it on Saturday. The time will be from eleven to one o'clock."

Maybe he had mentioned it to me. These days I was lucky enough to remember my middle name. The last thing I wanted to do was host an open house, but I had agreed to take the listing, and those things came with the territory. "Well, that's terrific."

He paused, the key in the doorknob. "No need for the sarcasm, darling. I'm showing houses starting at ten thirty, so I can't be there, but maybe one of the other agents can take it."

I wasn't sure I wanted that either, but said nothing as we entered and hung our coats on the brass hooks in the small foyer. The gray brick building was two levels and had required some cosmetics when Jacques bought it last year but was now as chic as he was. Jacques spared no expense in his clothing or furniture—two luxuries he allowed himself to indulge in. Heck, he worked hard for his money and was entitled.

Zoe's receptionist desk was a large mahogany L-shape. There was a separate room with a dark wood Tommy Bahama conference table that seated ten. The walls were all stark white with gray trim. A giant brick veneer archway separated the reception area and small sitting room from the conference room and Jacques' impressive office. There were four other offices located upstairs, including mine, and a communications room with stations for agents in training that was rarely used.

As we started toward Jacques' office, I heard a sudden high-pitched giggle from upstairs. My right eye started to twitch immediately. "Stacey's here?"

Jacques extended his palms up in the air. "She landed a new listing yesterday. My guess is that she's probably entering it on the computer."

I was sorely tempted to ask who Stacey had stolen it from but forced my tongue to remain silent. The listing leak in the office irritated Jacques to no end, so it was best not to bring it up. Stacey reminded me of another agent—one whose dead body I'd discovered last year. Neither woman would stop at anything to climb their way to the top. They enjoyed stepping on everyone who got in the way with their five-inch stiletto heels. This week it was Arial's office Stacey wanted. Maybe next week—my listings?

Before we could say anything further, Stacey appeared on the small staircase, cell phone glued to her ear. "I'm pretty sure I can get three hundred grand for it. It needs a new septic system, but hey, the buyers don't have to know that part." She giggled again then froze when she looked up and saw us standing near Zoe's desk.

"Hello, Jacques," Stacey said politely. Her lips curled back into a sneer when she spotted me. "Cindy."

Jacques sucked in some air and said nothing. One thing that he prided himself on in this business was honesty. His hands balled into fists at his sides as he waited for Stacey to end her conversation.

Stacey got the message. "Let me call you back," she said to the other party and promptly clicked off. She stood on the bottom step, waiting for Jacques to make the next move. The tension in the room was as thick as the lumps in the mashed potatoes Helen had fixed last night for dinner.

The young woman's cheeks flushed scarlet as she met Jacques' gaze, and then she gave him a gleaming smile. "I finished entering the listing for 24 Walter Avenue, Jacques. And guess what? I already have a showing scheduled for tomorrow afternoon. They seem pretty interested too."

Jacques pursed his lips together. "Stacey, if you're aware of a known defect with a house, you are required by law to make it known to all interested parties. To not do so is illegal, and I won't have that at my agency."

"Oh, right." She looked startled. "I'd never do that. I was talking about the other listing I have—you know, the one that's pending on Howard Lane. The structural and the termite inspections are scheduled for Monday, and I recommended to the buyers that they have the septic looked at, but they don't want to spend the money."

Skepticism shone through Jacques face like the sun. "Stacey, I hope that you're telling me the truth. Please make sure that you get this in writing so we're not liable."

"Oh, right. No worries." She twisted her long blonde hair around her fingers and smiled at him in a coy manner. "Um, I was wondering if you were free for dinner tonight? I have a couple of ideas for the house on Rodgers Way that I'd love to talk to you about."

Jacques gestured at me. "That's Cindy's listing."

"I know that." Her delicate nose wrinkled at me. "But I figured that Cindy would be out on maternity leave for a while and you'd need someone to help with it."

I almost wanted to laugh out loud but didn't dare. Stacey must be the only one in the office—or town—that didn't know Jacques was gay. Or perhaps she didn't want to face the truth. She was clearly attracted to him and had been trying unsuccessfully to put the moves on him since she'd come to work here three months ago.

Jacques' frown disappeared. "Stacey, do you happen to be free between eleven and one tomorrow?"

Her face brightened. "Why, yes, I am. What do you need me to—"

I tugged at Jacques' arm. "Can I speak to you in your office for a moment? *Alone?*"

He nodded. "I'll catch up with you later, Stacey. By the way, where's your car?"

Stacey smiled. "It's in the shop until Monday. I had a friend drop me off, but I'd love a ride home if you have the time."

The girl was so obvious. She needed to play a little harder to get—and with someone besides our boss, that is.

Poor Jacques' expression was pained. "Sorry, Stacey, I have to drive Cindy home."

"But I drove myself." I couldn't keep the grin off my face. "Remember?"

"I guess it's just you and me then, Jacques." She watched him with unbridled fascination. "I'll be ready to go whenever you are, boss."

We left her standing there and went into Jacques' office. He slumped in the leather chair behind his massive desk, while I eased myself into a chair beside it.

"Why'd you have to go and tell her that?" he groused.

"I wouldn't want to deprive her of the opportunity to try to seduce you for about the hundredth time this month," I chuckled.

He rolled his eyes in despair. "Do I have to spell it out for her?"

"Yes, I think that you do."

Jacques sighed, opened his desk drawer, and swallowed two Tylenol dry from the bottle. "What did you want to talk to me about?"

"I'll host the open house tomorrow." There was no way I was going to let Stacey within a mile of the Rodgers mansion.

Jacques' mouth twitched at the corners. "Really? Gee, what's the reason for your sudden change of heart?"

I glared back at him. "Oh, cut it out. You know as well as I do the woman is a pariah. I've already been down that road before, in case you've forgotten."

Jacques leaned forward across his desk. "Yes, I remember only too well. Listen, I appreciate this and realize that you don't want to keep leaving the baby. As soon as I'm done with my showings, I'll come and relieve you. Then again, I may not make it at all. The problem is that these are new clients of mine and they're being vague about how many houses they want to see. I have five lined up, but they said it depends on their mood." He closed his eyes and sighed dramatically.

"It's all right. Greg can give Grace a bottle if I'm not back in time. But I want you to know that no matter what happens, I am out the door at exactly one o'clock. I don't care if Brad Pitt shows up at 1:05—I will already be on my way home."

"Damn." Jacques breathed. "I'd show him a house anytime. The man is fine." He took off his glasses to polish them, placed them back on, and examined my face. "What's really bothering you?"

"Nothing," I lied. Yvette's words about my confused state popped back into my mind, but I didn't want to discuss it. I hated the fact that she'd been so accurate with her observations. I rose to my feet. "I need to get home. By the way, I think that Eleanor should tell Percy's siblings about the open house tomorrow."

He looked puzzled. "Don't you think that's rubbing more salt into their already open, money-hungry wounds?"

"Perhaps, but they may show up out of curiosity, and if they do, that would be the perfect opportunity for me to have a little chat with each one of them."

Jacques looked impressed. "You go, Jessica Fletcher."

"Hey, I'm not that old. *Yet*."

CHAPTER FOURTEEN

"Relax, sweetheart, I have everything under control." Greg took Grace from my arms and kissed me on the lips.

"There's a bottle of breast milk in the fridge, and I changed her a few minutes ago. She'll probably sleep until I get back." I was busy stuffing flyers for the open house into my briefcase. "What did I do with the sign-in sheet? Oh, there it is." I pulled it out from the middle of the flyers.

Greg smiled as he cradled Grace. "Stop worrying. I have done this a few times before, remember? We'll be fine until you get back. What are you afraid of—that I'll put her diaper on backwards?"

I lifted an eyebrow at him. "Well?"

"Okay, okay. It only happened once with Darcy. Hey, I was a newbie back then."

He looked so adorable with that sheepish grin on his face, similar to the twins when they'd done something wrong. I gave him another light peck on the lips. "See you in a couple of hours." I leaned down and gave our sleeping baby a kiss on her forehead then hurried out the front door, firmly biting my lower lip.

As I drove away from the house, I burst into tears. It was a relief to know that I'd managed to hide my feelings from both Greg and Jacques, but the truth of the matter was, something inside of me had changed since Grace was born. My priorities had shifted. I didn't want to be away from her and felt terrible running off each day, even if it was only for a couple of hours. Maybe I was experiencing some type of depression. I honestly wasn't sure. I'd felt like this to some degree after Darcy and the twins were born, but the sensation was more prominent this time.

Staying home full-time wasn't an option—I knew this. We needed the money, even though my sales had been nothing to brag about as of late. But I also knew I was pushing myself too hard too soon, and that was no one's fault but my own. Percy's dying request of me had been to find his killer. I wanted to help, but this was all too much for me right now. After today, I had to take a step back and hope that the police would be able to find out who had taken Percy's life.

I arrived at the house at 10:40, cutting it a bit close, but fortunately there were no cars waiting. Eleanor's rental was in the driveway with the motor running, and Jacques had come by earlier to place the *Open House* sign on the front lawn for me. Eleanor had offered to stay for the opening, but I didn't like for the owner to be present. Potential clients were turned off by it, and they tended not to linger and ask questions if they knew the owner was nearby.

I alighted from the car and grabbed my briefcase, relieved that the weather was cooperating for once. The temperature was above freezing today, and the ice from the recent storm had started to dissipate into puddles around my feet. Maybe spring wasn't too far away after all.

Eleanor met me at the front door. She was dressed in a

leather bomber jacket and jeans. Her face was drawn, and dark circles of weariness were noticeable underneath her eyes.

"Bad night?" I asked.

She frowned. "Every night that I spend in this house is a bad night. I've left a plate of cookies out on the dining room table that I made earlier this morning. I had someone come in the other day to clean but realize there are still things that will turn a potential buyer off. The condition of the floors, the water stain in the ceiling—"

"That doesn't mean you won't get a serious offer," I said. "If they really like the house, their agent will advise them to offer less because of these repairs."

"Well, that's fine with me," she retorted. "I only want to get back to California. Tom is very angry. When he found me with Diane yesterday, he practically threw me out of their home. I mentioned the open house to them, like you asked me to, and it was like striking a match to a puddle of gasoline." Her nostrils flared. "A very bad idea."

Yikes. "Did you get a chance to tell Andrew and his wife as well?"

She nodded. "I talked to Andrew. He's been acting very indifferent about the whole situation. He's angry too but handles it better. Unlike Tom and Diane, he and Brenda don't need the money."

"What does he do for a living?" I asked with interest.

"Andrew has his own private dental practice." She spoke with a note of sarcasm in her voice. "He always received more opportunities than Percy did. Brenda doesn't work and leads quite the pampered life. Between you and me, I think that Stella left the house to Percy instead of Andrew because she felt like Andrew was the privileged one, most likely to succeed, blah blah. Stella always had a passion for helping the underdog."

I placed my coat over one of the chairs surrounding the maple dining room table and started to arrange flyers on the surface. "After Percy moved into the house, did he ever tell you that he knew who the real killer was?"

Eleanor's eyes widened in shock then shifted to the wall behind me. "No, never. But like I said before, Stella may have known. Maybe she told Percy during one of her visits to the prison." Her lower lip trembled. "If Percy did discover the truth, it looks like it came a little too late to help him."

Maybe it wouldn't do any harm to let Eleanor in on my secret. "When Jacques and I were going through the boxes in the attic, we found a diary that belonged to Vanessa. One of the entries was quite disturbing. It read, 'If I leave him, he'll kill me.'"

Eleanor sucked in a breath. "Why would she write something like that?"

I shrugged. "I'm assuming she was concerned that Percy would find out about her alleged affair and try to murder her."

Her nostrils flared, and the color rose in her cheeks. "It wasn't alleged. Vanessa did sleep around on him. She even admitted it." She grabbed the back of the chair for support. "It's weird she would write something like that about him. Percy wasn't a violent man. He was against guns."

"But Vanessa wasn't shot," I said gently. "She was stabbed." What I wanted to say, but couldn't bring myself to, was that in the heat of an argument, he could have easily picked up a knife in the kitchen and killed her. "He also didn't have an alibi."

She pinned me with her gaze. "I thought you believed that Percy was innocent?"

"I do, but crimes of passion happen all the time."

Eleanor shook her head vehemently. "It's simply not true. He worshipped the ground she walked on." Anger flashed in her eyes. "All you're interested in is your commission."

That was when I realized it had been a mistake to tell her. I placed a hand on her arm. "Eleanor, that's not true. I want to know what happened as badly as you do. If we could—"

She shook my hand off. "For God's sake, just sell the damn

house so that I can get on with my life." With that, she turned and hurried toward the front door, slamming it behind her. In shock, I stood in the foyer as her car peeled out of the driveway, tires squealing. Did Eleanor know something that she had conveniently neglected to tell me?

I began to climb the stairs to the second floor, when the front door opened again. I turned back around and, upon reaching the great room, saw Tom Brenner coming toward me. His eyes scanned my body up and down as he drew closer, and a chill passed over me. He was unshaven, his dark hair uncombed, and the trench coat he wore rumpled, as if he'd been lying in a gutter somewhere. My face must have registered shock, because a huge smirk dominated his.

"Hoping for a big sale today?" he taunted.

I swallowed hard and gripped the bannister for support. "Hello, Mr. Brenner. What can I do for you?"

Tom ignored me as he walked into the great room. When he noticed the water spot on the ceiling, he laughed with contempt. "Guess that will take away a few bucks of your commission, huh? Maybe I should do a quick paint job. How much do you pay, sweetie?"

I didn't reply. Chards of ice settled in my bloodstream, and I didn't want to be alone with this man. He was bitter and potentially dangerous. Eleanor had mentioned that Tom and Diane had money problems. If Eleanor was out of the picture, could he and Diane claim the house? Did he hope that Eleanor might end up like Percy?

The front door opened, and to my relief, a man and woman who looked to be in their midthirties walked in. They were attractive and well dressed, the man carrying a toddler in his arms. I prayed fervently that Tom would not make a scene.

"Go ahead," he mocked, waving his hand forward in a dismissive manner. "Go get your sale, Mrs. York. Don't worry about me. I'll pretend to be a prospective buyer as well." He crossed to the stairs and started up, taking them two at a time, until he disappeared from my line of vision.

My pulse quickened. Should I follow him? If Eleanor figured that Stella might have left a clue in the house to the killer's identity, maybe there was a chance that others thought the same thing. By informing them know about the open house, I may have inadvertently taken away my opportunity to discover any clues before they did.

A murmur of soft voices came from the foyer, and I hurried over to the couple. "Hello," I greeted them. "I'm Cindy York from Forte Realty."

"Rob and Gina Swisher," the man replied and held out his hand to me. "This is our daughter, Ashley."

I smiled at the little girl who had started to wriggle in his arms. "Hi, Ashley. It's nice to meet you."

"Is it okay if we go ahead and look around?" Gina asked.

"Please do." I pointed through the archway to the dining room, located on the opposite side of the great room. "If you could sign in first, that would be great. The clipboard is on the table." I smiled at the little girl. "There are chocolate chip cookies in there as well. Feel free to let me know if you have questions or need anything."

Before I could even start toward the stairs, the front door opened again. Damn! I turned around and was relieved to see Susan Redwood standing there. She was an agent with Houses Galore. This meant that Susan either had a client with her or was checking the house out first before she brought someone in for a showing. At least I wouldn't have to babysit her. The longer Tom was left alone upstairs, the more anxious I became.

Susan's face broke into a wide smile when she spotted me. She was an attractive woman in her early sixties with a mass of curly salt-and-pepper hair and warm brown eyes. "Hi, Cindy. I thought this might be your listing, but your name plate isn't on the sign yet."

"Thanks for coming by, Susan. No, it only went on the market this past week, and I haven't had a chance to add my plate yet. Do you have clients with you?"

She nodded. "They're meeting me here." She glanced past me into the great room. "It needs some work, huh? Do you think the owner would be willing to negotiate?"

Typical agent lingo, which translated into, "How much will they come down?" I wasn't playing that game—yet. "I really can't comment. Like I said, it only came on the market a couple of days ago."

Susan shot me a disbelieving look. "Come on. Everyone knows there was a murder here. No one's going to offer what you're asking. It's way too high."

Exasperated, I gritted my teeth. "Susan, this house has great bones, and the work it needs is minor." Okay, maybe I was exaggerating a bit. "If you're looking for a clearance sale, you've come to the wrong place."

She stared at me, startled, and for a second I was too. It was hard to believe that I'd spoken those words aloud. It wasn't my nature to be so bold, but there wasn't time to fool around. I had more important issues to deal with upstairs.

The Swishers were in the kitchen, so this seemed like a good time to take my leave. I excused myself to Susan and hurried up the stairs. There were three bedrooms on the second floor, and the third floor held an additional two. The fourth floor—the attic—was where Jacques and I had spent a good deal of time yesterday. I checked the bedrooms on the second floor plus the bathrooms, but Tom wasn't there. He must be on the third floor in Stella's lair.

I took the stairs at a slower pace this time. My incision had started to hurt, and I was exhausted, both mentally and physically. This listing was not helping my frame of mind either. Maybe I should have let Stacey help. I hated to do it, but something had to give.

The wooden windowsills were chipped in Stella's bedroom and needed staining, while the once white walls were a sallow yellow color. The door was open, so I peered in. Tom was standing by the canopy bed, checking something on his phone. His back was to me.

It was a simple room, only about 12x14 in size, but the old-fashioned wood trim on the walls and the high ceiling gave it a certain charm. The canopy bed was covered with a white lace duster, and a variety of decorative pillows sat at the head. There was an antique-looking washstand, an old-fashioned mahogany armoire, and a matching nightstand. As I watched, Tom put away his phone and walked over to some assorted pictures on the nightstand. He lifted one, snorted back a laugh, and then put the photo back down. He must have sensed my presence behind him because he suddenly whirled around. His eyes shot daggers across the room at me.

"What's the matter?" he taunted. "Afraid that I'll steal something?"

"Of course not," I lied and stepped into the room. "But there will be guests coming up shortly, so I wanted to see what—"

He came toward me, his dark eyes smoldering with uncontained anger. "Listen, Miss Fancy Pants Real Estate Agent. I don't know who the hell you think you are, but this house should have been mine and Diane's. I suppose Eleanor told you that Stella never liked me, huh? In fact, she begged Diane not to marry me. To attempt to get even, she deliberately cut us out of her will and gave the mansion to that murdering brother of Diane's. Pure spite, I tell you."

"Why didn't she like you?" Gee, this was difficult to imagine. Tom had such a winning personality.

"I overheard her tell Diane once that I was a low-down letch who was only after the family money." Tom clenched his fists at his sides. "She had other ideas about me as well."

"Like what?" I asked. "Did she think you were having an affair with Vanessa?"

His nostrils flared, and he took a step closer to me as I silently cursed myself. Why was it that the older I got, the less of a filter my mouth had?

"That's insane," he rasped out. "How dare you say such a thing to me."

Cold stark fear settled in the bottom of my stomach, but there was no way I'd let him know that I was afraid of him. "Perhaps it would be best if you left now."

Tom clamped his lips together. "I'll leave when I'm damn good and ready. Not that it's any of your business, but I didn't kill Percy. I wasn't having an affair with Vanessa either. But from what I've heard, she had plenty of partners, both male *and* female."

Was he making this up to gauge my reaction? I decided not to play along. "Whatever you say."

My indifference seemed to make him even angrier. "Come on. What are you really doing? Are you here to sell a house or to solve a murder? I know about your reputation."

My mouth opened in surprise. "What exactly do you know?"

His lips curled back into a sneer. "That you and your boss have been involved in some past murder investigations. I did a search for you on Google. A former co-worker of yours died, and you were under suspicion for her killing. Then you helped prove that a former friend didn't commit suicide years ago but was murdered instead." He put his hands together in a mock clap. "Jessica Fletcher in the making."

Cripes. If I was constantly going to be compared to a fictional detective, couldn't it be Nancy Drew? Too bad I was more than twice her age. "Percy told me who killed him, right before he died."

The words fell out of my mouth before I could stop them. Perhaps I secretly hoped that by saying the words out loud, Tom would make a confession. When I saw the look on his face, however, I realized my mistake.

"You're a liar," he whispered, and took another step forward.

So much for my defiant attitude. The crazed look in his eyes had started to scare me, and I found my feet frozen to the floor. By the time I was able to move and start for the doorway, he pushed me backward. To my amazement, he slammed the door shut and then shoved my body up against it. His hand came up and pinned both my arms against the door. His face was so close to mine that I could smell his undesirable breath, which reeked of alcohol. Drunk before noon on a Saturday. How charming.

In a panic, I struggled to free myself. "Let go of me."

His hands were like steel, and I couldn't budge them. "Not until you tell me what you know."

My brain had gone numb, and I didn't know what to do next. There were potential buyers walking around downstairs, and I didn't want to make a scene, but this guy was terrifying me. I continued to struggle. "Take your hands off me!" I shrieked.

Tom placed a hand over my mouth, and I bit him.

"Ouch! You stupid bitch!" He raised a hand in the air, as if to strike me. At that moment there was a knock on the door, and we both froze.

CHAPTER FIFTEEN

"Cindy?" Jacques' worried voice carried from the other side of the door, and he rattled the knob. "What are you doing in there?"

"Help me, Jacques!" I screamed before Tom covered my mouth again.

The door started to inch open slowly, despite our bodies pressed against it. Tom released his hand from my mouth in an attempt to shut it, and at that split second, the door flew open, knocking both of us to the floor.

Jacques was immediately at my side, helping me up. "Are you all right?"

Relieved, I leaned against him as he placed an arm around my shoulders to support me. "Yes, now that you're here."

Jacques shut the door and turned back around, his face suffused with fury. Tom had managed to get to his feet, a bit unsteady, his drunken state more pronounced now.

"How dare you lay a finger on her," Jacques said angrily.

Tom lifted his middle finger in salute. "Get over it. Your little helper is fine. I didn't do anything to her. She was threatening *me.*"

A muscle ticked in Jacques' jaw, and his skin turned the color of a forest fire. He looked at me. "What really happened, Cin?"

Gingerly I rubbed my arms. "He covered my mouth with his hand and pinned me against the door. I thought he was going to hit me."

Before I could even finish the last sentence, Jacques' fist had already connected with Tom's mouth. The man fell to the floor, groaning and swearing profusely.

I screamed and grabbed Jacques by the arm, but he shook me off. "Back up, Cin. Let me finish the job."

"No!" I panicked. "This will only make things worse!"

"Cindy?" Susan's voice resonated from the hallway. "Is everything okay in there?"

Crap. Jacques and I exchanged a panicked glance as Tom managed to get to his feet. He was bleeding profusely from either the nose or mouth. I couldn't tell which one.

Jacques tossed him a handkerchief. "There. Now get the hell out of here."

Tom mopped at his face with the cloth and presented us with a malicious smile. "You're both going to be sorry that you tangled with me. I'll press charges."

Jacques' mouth set in a firm, hard line. "Go right ahead. And I'll be sure to tell the police how you assaulted this woman."

Tom muttered a four-letter expletive under his breath then yanked the door open. Susan was standing there, her mouth open wide enough for a canary to fly into. Tom pushed past her, and a moment later we heard him thundering down the stairs. The front door slammed a second later.

Susan clutched a clipboard to her chest. "Are you two all right?"

Jacques shook his hand out, which was visibly swelling. "Everything is fine. The man came to look at the house and got a little too friendly with Cindy."

Susan made a *tsk-tsk* sound and shook her head. "The same

thing happened to me last week. Such a world we live in. They all want us for our bodies."

My eyebrows rose before I could stop them. Jacques gave Susan a funny look but didn't comment.

Her gaze came to rest on his hand, and I saw her eyes widen. "Oh my, your hand is all swollen. What happened, Jacques?"

"Bee sting," I said quickly.

Now it was Susan's turn for disbelief. "In February?"

Homina homina homina. "Um," I hedged. "Jacques recently got back from Florida."

Jacques rolled his eyes toward the ceiling. "God help me," he whispered. "Never mind. Bring your clients in, Susan."

"Ladies." Susan called out into the hallway. "Come say hello to Cindy."

For some unexplainable reason, my right eye started to twitch like it did when I was around Helen. I should have known that was not a good sign, a premonition of sorts. Sure enough, two elderly women appeared in the doorway, and I did my best not to groan. Fate was definitely not my friend today.

"Hello, ladies." I tried to sound cheerful, but my voice was still subdued after what had happened with Tom.

The women both gave Jacques their best sunshiny smiles then glowered at me. Lila and Gloria Danson were sisters, in their late sixties or early seventies. Although siblings, they were complete opposites as far as looks were concerned. Lila was thick waisted with shoulder-length, fine white hair, while her sister Gloria was tiny and possessed a short, curly silver bob.

Every time I had a listing, I somehow managed to encounter these two women, who had been on a quest for a new home for what seemed like an eternity. I'd last crossed paths with them at an open house for a client whose brother had been a close friend of mine.

Lila ran her tongue over her lips and pointed at me. "Susan

warned us that you had the listing on this house. But we wanted to see it anyway."

I bristled inwardly at the comment but said nothing.

"Where's Sherlock?" Jacques asked. They never went anywhere without their brown, untrained bulldog. He liked me about as much as his owners did. I could almost envision him peeing in one of the bedrooms downstairs with the Swishers looking on in horror and their toddler giggling, "Look what the puppy did, Mommy!"

Gloria tossed her head in an arrogant manner. "He's out in the car with our chauffeur."

The real kicker was that the sisters had won the lottery last year and could afford any home they desired. Susan was practically foaming at the mouth to sell them one.

"We thought it was better if he stayed there," Lila agreed. "He doesn't like you very much."

I grinned so wide that my cheeks started to hurt. "If you ladies will excuse me, I need to go see how the other couple is getting on downstairs."

"Oh, they already left." Susan jerked her head toward the hallway. "Cindy, can I speak to you in private for a moment?"

Intrigued, I stared over at Jacques, who shooed me away with his hand. "Go ahead. I've got it covered." He gave the women his most gracious smile and extended an arm to each one of them. "Let me show you the rest of the floor, ladies."

Gloria and Lila both giggled and wasted no time in attaching themselves to Jacques. "My goodness, Mr. Forte. We should blow this joint and go tie one on together," Lila said.

"Do you like older women?" Gloria asked.

Good grief. I went out into the hallway with Susan tagging after me, and we started down the stairs together. "What's it like having those two for clients?" I asked. "They've only been looking at houses for what—forever now?"

Susan groaned in despair. "Don't remind me. They're driving me nuts. I've shown them 95 houses. Ninety-five!"

"Do you get a gold star when you reach one hundred?" I couldn't help myself.

She sucked in a breath at my snide comment. "Oh, that's hilarious. Actually, I think they enjoy looking at homes and trying to nose around into other people's business. Lookie loos, or *kookie* loos, take your pick. If they don't buy a house soon, I may do something drastic."

And I thought I had problems. "Well, maybe they'll want to offer on this one."

"That's what I wanted to talk to you about." Susan paused. "They did mention that they really like the place. By the way, the other couple left before you screamed, so don't think that you scared them away."

That was a relief. "Did they say anything to you?"

She shook her head. "Not directly, but I did overhear them talking on the phone to someone. It must have been their agent. They said something about coming back for another look."

My heart gave a little jolt. Maybe there was a silver lining to this day after all. "Good to know."

"Okay, now that I've shared some pleasant news, level with me in return," Susan said. "How much is the new owner willing to come down in price?"

Her candor didn't come as a surprise, and I merely shrugged. "Susan, I have no idea. It's only been on the market for a few days. There's been a lot going on with this house, as you already know."

Susan pursed her lips. "The new owner doesn't even live in the area, so she must be anxious to unload it. By the way, I saw her with Mr. Rodgers' sister yesterday. They were having dinner at the Casa Café." Her mouth formed a sly grin. "They were also having a very heated conversation."

Now she had my attention. "You know Percy's sister?"

Susan flashed me an arrogant smile. "Not personally, but I know who Diane Brenner is. That was her husband who ran out of here after Jacques hit him. You're not fooling me, Cindy. He's upset about the house, isn't he? He thinks they got stiffed."

This was all that I needed right now. Susan had a mouth the size of a great white shark. "That's really none of your business."

The woman was practically salivating in anticipation. "Don't worry. I'd never kiss and tell. *If* you let me in on how much Miss Cassidy is willing to go down in price, that is."

Sure, she didn't kiss and tell. Her gossip might happen to make the front page of the local paper tomorrow morning, or at the very least, Homes Galore's Facebook page. The real estate market was getting so corrupt lately that it had started to sicken me. Maybe that was another reason for my sudden change of heart.

Oh hell. There was no reason why I couldn't tell her. "Fine. You win. She'll go down at least fifty grand."

Susan's smile faded. "That's *all*?"

"Well jeez, Susan, she's not going to give it away!"

Her expression was forlorn. "I figured with Mr. Rodgers' murder and all, that it might work in my favor. At least a hundred grand, maybe even more."

"You know that the murder doesn't have to be disclosed to potential buyers," I said. "Now, tell me what you overheard at the restaurant."

Susan's face brightened. "Well, I heard Diane telling Miss Cassidy that she'd had it with her husband. Tom, right? She said she should have divorced him years ago. And Eleanor said something like, yeah, well, why did you stop the proceedings back then? Then Diane got kind of flustered and said you know damn well why. After that, Eleanor clammed up. I missed a bit when the waiter came over, and then Diane said something like, wow, you're loving this, aren't you? So is Andrew."

My pulse quickened. What exactly was going on here? If

Diane and Tom were going to divorce years ago, why didn't they go through with it? What or who had changed their minds at the last minute?

With Susan waiting for my reaction, I tried not to reveal my true feelings. "Ah, it might not mean anything."

She gave me a disbelieving look. "Fine. Have it your own way."

"Miss Redwood!" Lila's voice boomed from the top of the stairs. "We want to talk to you. *Now*."

Susan closed her eyes for a second, as if trying to gain her bearings. "Sweet Lord. Please excuse me while I go rejoin the loony sisters."

As she ascended the staircase, I checked the other rooms, but no one else had come in during our absence. It was time to put Susan's eavesdropping to the test and hope that my good friend Marcia Steele would help me out.

Marcia was a real estate attorney who I recommended to all my clients. We'd worked together on several occasions. She was honest, fair, and one of the best in the business at doing title searches. I pulled my phone out and pressed the button for her number. Since it was a Saturday I decided to try her cell first. It rang twice before she picked up.

"Why hello, new mommy," she greeted me. "Congratulations on the addition to the York family. What did you end up naming her?"

I smiled. "Her name is Grace. And thank you for the beautiful flowers. I've been meaning to send you a card, but things have been a bit crazy lately."

She sounded concerned. "Is everything okay with your little bundle of joy?"

"Oh yes, she's fine, thanks. It's the real estate end of things that I'm having issues with."

Marcia's tone became puzzled. "You're back to work already? What kind of a slave driver is Jacques turning into these days? I know the business isn't exactly booming, but the man has to ease up."

I laughed. "It's not Jacques' fault. I happened on a new listing right before I went into labor."

"I haven't heard from you or Jacques in quite a while about a deal. Did you go off and get yourself a new attorney? The truth now."

Her mannerism was light and teasing, but I knew she had to be curious. "You know I'd never do that. Everyone's sales are down, but ours seem to be even worse. Between you and me, we're afraid that there might be a leak in the office somewhere. That's not why I'm calling, though. I did an open house for my new listing at 25 Rodgers Way. Thc former owner, Percy Rodgers, was murdered there last week."

Marcia exhaled sharply. "Good God, Cindy, I read all about that. They said his real estate agent found him. Please tell me that wasn't you."

"Guilty as charged," I admitted.

"Unreal," she muttered in apparent disbelief. "Did someone put a curse on your head? I mean, what does this make, like the third or fourth body you've been involved with in the past year?"

My dead body count was higher than my house sales. "Yeah, I'm like the Pied Piper of homicide lately. Again, that's not why I'm calling. I need some legal information."

She was silent for a moment. "What sort of information? You know I can't divulge details about a client. Although for the record, Percy was never a client of mine."

"It's not about real estate. Someone told me that Percy's sister Diane and her husband Tom Brenner filed for divorce once but never went through with it. I was wondering if one of them might have used your husband. Patrick's been practicing for what, about twenty-five years now?"

"You have a good memory." Marcia sounded impressed.

"Actually, it will be 25 years next month. He passed the bar a few weeks before his 25th birthday. Which reminds me. I've got to start planning his big 5-0 party soon. We'll be next to reach that plateau, kiddo."

Something else to look forward to. *Not.* "Could you possibly check with Patrick and see if he knows anything? And if so, when this might have occurred?"

She sounded puzzled. "Well, it's up to Patrick, but I guess there's no harm in telling you that. Can I ask why you're so interested?"

"I'm curious if the date might coincide with the murder of Percy's wife Vanessa," I explained. "There are a lot of bad feelings among the siblings."

"Well, why wouldn't there be?" she asked. "I mean, first Percy gets the house, and then he dies and it goes to someone who isn't even a relative? Frankly, I'd be pissed off myself."

"Can they contest the will?" I asked.

"Sure, they can contest it. Have they given any indication that they might?"

I cleared my throat. "I'm not sure what you mean by indication, but Percy's brother-in-law came to the open house I'm hosting today and tried to physically attack me." God help me, I did not want to tell Greg about this. Like Jacques, he'd try to rearrange Tom's face. "He wants that house and doesn't care how he has to go about getting it."

"Damn," Marcia breathed. "I hope you called the police."

I bypassed her question. "I don't believe Percy killed his wife, and I definitely don't want to attract any more attention to the house right now. For the time being I'm trying to check things out on my own."

"You go, Jessica Fletcher," she teased. "I'll check with Patrick and let you know what I find out."

Again with the Jessica Fletcher comments? Was this some type of conspiracy? "I appreciate it. Thanks so much, Marcia."

After I clicked off, I walked by the front window in the foyer and noticed that another vehicle had pulled in behind my car and Jacques'. A man and woman alighted from their black Jaguar, and I blinked twice when I realized who it was.

Andrew and Brenda Rodgers strolled hand in hand toward the front door of the house.

CHAPTER SIXTEEN

I had no one to blame except myself. The Rodgers family members were descending on me like a pack of vultures. Yes, I had asked Eleanor to tell the siblings about the open house, but somehow I hadn't quite envisioned it turning out this way.

To their credit, they knocked before they entered. I repositioned myself by the dining room table, as if checking the sign-in sheet. They both stomped snow from their boots and spoke to each other in low voices. I forced a smile to my lips as I approached them.

"Hello, Cindy." Brenda reached out a delicate cold hand for me to shake. "I hope it's okay that we stopped by."

Andrew raised an eyebrow. "Of course it's okay, my dear. This will always be *our* house, not Eleanor's. I don't give a damn about what my grandmother's will said. It makes no difference."

Great. It appeared I had another sore loser on my hands. Well, I wasn't playing ball. "If you'll excuse me, I have clients upstairs."

Andrew seemed surprised. "There are actually people interested in buying this place? It needs too much work."

"It's one of the oldest homes in the area," I said. "Victorian mansions are rich in history, and sometimes people don't care how much work is involved. There's a lot of charm and memories in this house."

He laughed bitterly. "Oh, that's hilarious. Yeah, there's a lot of charm in this house. Did you know that my parents pushed Percy and me off on our grandmother every summer? That's right. They wanted to go backpacking through Europe, like a couple of teenagers without any responsibilities, so they'd send us here. Wonderful and caring Grandma Stella could be a tough one to deal with at times. She'd have us up at the crack of dawn every day doing her bidding—washing windows, mowing the lawn, you name it. Nothing was ever done to her satisfaction either. She wouldn't hesitate to whack your butt with a belt if you smart-mouthed her or refused to do the work, believe me. Granny Rodgers was one tough cookie."

I winced at the mental image Andrew had portrayed of his grandmother. For some reason, I hadn't envisioned Stella like that. The picture I'd seen upstairs in her bedroom was one of a delicate, white-haired elderly woman with a sweet face and loving smile. Despite Helen's faults, she'd never struck my children, and if I ever found differently, there would be hell to pay.

Since Andrew had given me an opening, I decided to take it. "Did Percy get beaten too?"

Andrew seemed surprised by my question. "Once in a while, but it was mostly me."

Brenda added her two cents. "We were hurt when we found out she didn't leave us anything."

Andrew raised an eyebrow at his wife. "You know it wasn't about the house, dear. It was the principle of the whole thing. I don't give a damn about the money."

"That's true. We have lots," Brenda said proudly.

The look Andrew gave his wife could have formed icicles in

the room. He turned away from her, disdain evident on his face. "Is your associate here? The guy you came to the wake with?"

"Jacques? Yes, he's upstairs with some potential clients. Did you want to see him?"

Andrew addressed his wife. "Why don't you run on upstairs, darling, and tell Jacques that Betsy and Matt are looking for a place. They always loved dear, sweet Granny's house." His tone practically dripped with sarcasm.

"That's a great idea, honey." Brenda beamed and gaily trotted toward the stairs in her leather Gucci boots.

Andrew waited until his wife was out of earshot and then turned back to me. "Why are you so interested in all this? From what Eleanor told us, you didn't even want to represent Percy."

Heat rose through my face. "I was pregnant at the time and afraid the stress wouldn't be good for the baby. Eleanor asked me to reconsider, and I felt some type of moral obligation to Percy. Anyhow, you said you don't even care about the house."

He shrugged. "I don't. A word of advice, though. Stay away from my brother-in-law, Tom. He's pissed as hell that Diane didn't inherit the place."

"Too late," I said dryly. "You just missed him. For the record you're correct—he's definitely not happy."

Andrew's mouth dropped open. "What did he do to you?"

For some reason, I decided not to tell him about the incident. "Nothing," I lied. "Like you said, he basically complained that the house should have been his."

Andrew nodded in understanding. "He seems to think that because Eleanor has always been so close to Diane that she would have cut her in for a share. But that's not about to happen. The old broad is only concerned with one person —herself."

I leaned against the front door. "You don't like Eleanor?"

He gave me an arrogant smile. "Wow, are all real estate agents as nosy as you?"

For some reason, I laughed. At least this guy didn't seem abusive like Tom. Okay, it was obvious that his wife was lacking in the brain department and he'd probably married Brenda for her looks, but that wasn't my business. I was only concerned with justice for Percy.

"In answer to your question, yes, I'd say that all real estate agents are nosy. We interact with people constantly. That's how we make our money."

"Fair enough," Andrew said. "No, I don't particularly like Eleanor and never have. She's no relation to us, yet she's always managed to insert herself into our lives. The way she used my grandmother was pathetic."

I didn't like what he was implying. "What do you mean?"

Andrew's phone beeped. He pulled it out of his coat, checked the screen, typed out a message, and then returned it to his pocket. "Sorry. That was my office. A patient broke a tooth this morning. Looks like I'll be having office hours after all." He uttered a sigh of impatience. "What were we talking about? Oh right. Eleanor. I always felt that she attached herself to my grandmother because of her money."

"You think that Eleanor was using Stella?"

He gave me one of those *are you kidding* looks. "Please. Don't insult my intelligence. Gram gave her countless loans over the years, and from what I know, she never paid them back. Hey, it's none of my business. That was Gram's money to do with as she pleased. But once she got sick, Eleanor insisted on helping to take care of her. She flew out here several times over the past few years, and I know damn well she never paid for the airfare. Gram made her executor of her will and gave her access to her bank accounts. I have every reason to believe that Eleanor helped herself to my grandmother's dough—several times."

This discussion was leaving a very bad taste in my mouth. I didn't know what Eleanor's motive could have been for wanting

Vanessa dead, but it was obvious what killing Percy would have resulted in—her ownership of the mansion.

"Wow, that's terrible," I remarked, not knowing what else to say.

Andrew shrugged. "Like I said, the money isn't a big issue, but it pisses me off that Eleanor hasn't even offered to give Diane a share. Diane's always looked to her as a second mother, and I don't enjoy seeing my sister used like that."

"What about Percy? You don't seem very sorry that he's dead." *Oops.* My filterless mouth had taken over again.

Andrew didn't seem upset by my question. He placed his hands inside his coat pockets and stared out the colored pane of glass over the front door. "I'm sorry about a lot of things. I'm sorry we were never close and that I didn't help him when he needed it. But I can't change those things now, so what's the point in looking back?"

"Can I ask what happened between the two of you?"

He gave me a grim smile. "Percy made a pass at my girlfriend."

This was about the last thing I had expected to hear. "Was this while he was married to Vanessa?"

Andrew nodded. "Look, it's not something that I love talking about. He was drunk, and I punched him. Shortly afterward, Vanessa was found with her throat cut. We never saw it coming."

My head was spinning. None of this made any sense. "But Vanessa was the one who was having the affair."

Andrew shrugged. "What can I tell you? Things aren't always as they appear. He may have loved her, but that didn't stop him from trying to get a little extra on the side, if you know what I mean."

"Do you have any idea who Vanessa was having an affair with?" I asked.

His jaw dropped in amazement. "Are you an actual real

estate agent or pretending to be one? Because frankly, you're sticking your nose where it doesn't belong."

"Look," I said. "When I found Percy, his last words were about Vanessa. He told me how much he loved her. He asked me to help find her killer."

Andrew studied me for a second. "Yes, I heard that you found him. What else did he say?"

"Percy said that he didn't kill her."

He heaved a sigh of impatience. "Of course he'd say that. Why would he admit to killing his own wife?"

"He was dying. Why *not* admit it?" This guy was starting to irritate me. "What did he have to lose at that point?"

"Look, I'm sorry if I sound heartless," Andrew said. "I truly regret that my brother is dead, but we haven't been close since we were kids. After the fight we were even more distant than ever. My grandmother—the one person in our lives who seemed to give a damn about us—turned her back on everyone except Percy when he went to jail, including me. I came over here constantly to visit when she was sick, and what did she do? She up and left everything to my brother. Do you know how that made me feel?"

"No, I suppose I don't." The man was getting agitated, so I decided to change the subject. "What happened to your girlfriend? The one Percy made a pass at?"

"We broke up shortly after Vanessa was murdered. I think the whole thing with Percy made her nervous, and she worried that I might end up being abusive to her—or worse. You know, the whole *it must run in the family* type of behavior." He leaned against the wall. "It wasn't meant to be, but as they say, everything happens for a reason because then I found Brenda." He smiled as she waved to him from the top of the stairs.

"Do you have any kids?"

He shook his head. "No, but she wants them desperately. Brenda's thirty-eight, twelve years younger than me. She's been bugging me about adoption lately, but she still has some time to have one of her own. Heck, you're what—almost fifty? And you just had one."

I gritted my teeth but managed a smile. "I'm not quite there —*yet*. But thanks for the compliment."

My sarcasm was lost on Andrew as he watched his wife descend the staircase. "Brenda might be slow about certain things, but she's a good woman. She does a lot of charity work, and that kind of stuff benefits my career." He took her hand as she came over to him and brought it to his lips. "Ready to go, my love?"

"Yes, dear." Brenda turned and held out her other hand to me. "It was good to see you again, Cindy."

"Likewise. You two enjoy your day," I said.

Andrew gave me a polite nod. "Nice talking to you. Good luck with the house. You'll need it," he added as he opened the door for Brenda, and I shut it behind them.

I stood and watched as they walked toward their expensive car, Andrew's arm snug around Brenda's waist. Something wasn't sitting well in the bottom of my stomach, besides the bacon and egg sandwich I'd eaten earlier this morning. Andrew and Brenda's relationship reeked of phoniness. He seemed more interested in his wife's looks and appeal to the public than her actual intelligence. What if Brenda's flighty blonde act wasn't really an act after all?

My thoughts returned to the fistfight between Andrew and Percy. Was there any way to find this former girlfriend of Andrew's? Perhaps there was more to Brenda Rodgers than met the eye. Had she known Vanessa? She would have only been 17 or 18 when Vanessa died, and according to my knowledge—with the help of the newspaper articles—they hadn't married for another five years. If I were to pay a call on her while Andrew was at work, would she tell me anything? Probably not. She'd definitely blab all to her husband, and then another member of the Rodgers clan would hate me. But I was learning to live with that.

My conversation with Andrew had left me more confused than ever. Was there a chance Percy had really murdered his wife? If so, who had killed *him*?

CHAPTER SEVENTEEN

After we had seen the Danson sisters and Susan off, Jacques and I went to the kitchen in search of some ice for his hand. I found a plastic bag in one of the cabinets, filled it with cubes, and then gave it to him. We sat down at the small round oak table while he applied it to his hand. "Does it hurt much?"

He shrugged. "It stings a little, but the pain was well worth it. If that bastard ever tries to come near you again—"

"My knight in shining armor," I teased then grew serious. "Thank you for coming to my rescue. It means more than you know."

He looked at me solemnly. "There isn't anything I wouldn't do for you, Cin."

"Same here." We both fell silent and listened as the wall clock ticked away at the precious minutes of our lives. "You've already saved my life twice. I hope there won't be a third time."

Jacques studied my face. "You're thinking about the cards that Yvette read, aren't you? Specifically, the one that said someone was going to die."

I tried to shrug it off. "Come on. That's ridiculous."

"Ridiculous or not, we have to call the police and file charges against that psycho. He can't go around harassing women like that."

"No!" I spoke sharply. "If we do, he'll tell them that you started it. He could press charges against you as well. Tom may have grabbed me, but *you* punched him."

Jacques mouth set in a firm, hard line. "I don't care what he tells them. No one is going to treat you like that. What do you think Greg's reaction will be when he finds out? You are planning to tell him, I hope?"

"Yes. I'm not going to keep it a secret." Greg would take it about as well as Jacques had. "Remember what we said—about doing anything for each other?" My voice choked up. "I know that things are really rough for you right now, and this incident with Tom is something else you don't need to deal with. Yes, he grabbed me and put his hand over my mouth, but he didn't hit me, and I don't want to see this hurt you. Please let it go." Much to my dismay, tears started to sting my eyes.

Startled, Jacques put a hand on my arm. "Hey. What's going on? This isn't like you. Are you acting this way because of the baby? Post-pregnancy bliss?"

I snorted back a laugh and wiped at my eyes. "It's called post-partum depression. I have an appointment to talk to my doctor in a couple of days, but don't think that's the issue. What if I don't want this anymore?"

Jacques squeezed my hand. "It's always been your dream to sell a million-dollar house, love. At least ever since I've known you."

"Exactly. I've been in the business for over four years. I've come close a couple of times, but close doesn't cut it. How many million-dollar houses have you sold, compared to my zero?"

Jacques started counting on his fingers. When he went around the second time, I stopped him. "Okay, point well taken. Since I had Grace, my priorities have changed. I've been thinking about what's really important in this life to me, and real estate is at the bottom of the list. It's after Greg, the kids, our pets, and you."

"Wow, I come after the pets? I'm flattered," he teased.

I rolled my eyes. "You know what I mean. Yes, I love real estate and interacting with the public, but I'm not a natural like you are."

"You're a very good agent, darling," Jacques assured me. "Don't sell yourself short. See, I can make funnies too."

"Hilarious."

He patted my hand. "I had a feeling you might say something like that. Listen, I don't mean to pry into your financial situation, but don't you guys really need the money?"

"We do." I heaved a sigh of impatience. "So, it's out of the question for now."

"Don't worry, love. We'll figure out something." Jacques glanced at his watch. "It's one o'clock, so we can officially close up shop, and you can return home to that precious cargo of yours."

My phone beeped, and I glanced down at the screen. It was a text message from Eleanor, and I groaned as I read it. "Eleanor wants to know if we can wait a few minutes. She's on her way back and would like to talk to both of us. She said it will take about 15 minutes for her to get here."

Jacques heaved himself out of the chair. "Well, let's not waste time. Are you up for some more snooping in the attic? Or did you plan to put your Jessica Fletcher detective license away forever too?"

I shot him a death glare. "Stop calling me that. God knows I feel old enough already. No, I have a better idea. Let's search Stella's room."

His green eyes widened in surprise. "What exactly are you looking for?"

"I'm not sure," I confessed. "But I keep thinking about what

Eleanor told us that day at the wake, remember? How Stella said the answer was with the cards."

Jacques shrugged. "Well, she believed in tarot. That's not unusual."

We started to climb the staircase together. "Yes, but what if she meant something else? You told me yourself that Yvette couldn't determine who the killer was, so what would the cards tell us then?"

A fine line deepened between his eyebrows. "What are you suggesting? That we go back up to the attic and check all the decks of cards again?"

"I'm betting that if one of the decks did hold a clue, we won't find it in the attic. Stella would have kept them close to her."

"The woman had dementia," Jacques pointed out. "I've heard that people who suffer from it sometimes hide things in strange places. The cards might be in the attic, or maybe not. It's a shot in the dark."

We reached the third floor and went into Stella's bedroom. I was tired from climbing the stairs and my earlier run-in with Tom. Jacques looked beat as well. He always dressed to impress, but today he couldn't carry it off. Jacques' hand was still red and swollen, his tie askew, trousers wrinkled, and he had a fine beard of scruff growing around his mouth, as if he hadn't shaved in a few days.

"Anything new with Ed?" I tried to keep my tone casual.

He shook his head. "We were supposed to have dinner together last night, but he ended up having to cover for someone at the restaurant. Who am I kidding? He's never going to meet me halfway."

"Don't say that. If you love each other, things can be worked out."

"Ah, Cynthia." He looked slightly amused as we stood in front of the armoire. "Such a romantic at heart. You want everyone to be as much in love as you and Greg are. By the way, what are you and hubby doing for Valentine's Day? It's coming up soon."

I shrugged. "Probably nothing. Like you, we have so much spare time on our hands these days."

Feeling a bit like a thief, I started to rummage through the drawers in Stella's nightstand while Jacques opened the mahogany doors of the armoire and searched through the clothes inside. The nightstand drawers didn't hold any items of interest. There were some books, underwear, and a few old pictures, several which were in black and white. I came across a colored photo of Percy and Vanessa at their wedding—the same one that had been featured in the newspapers—and another from Tom and Diane's.

"I'm not finding anything in here," Jacques complained.

"Maybe my hunch was wrong." I sat down on Stella's bed, with a copy of a black leather Bible in my hands. "She knew who killed Vanessa, I'm almost positive. Why she chose *not* to tell though, I don't understand."

"We need to face the facts here, Cin," Jacques said. "Stella may have known that Percy killed Vanessa. That could be the reason why she chose never to reveal it."

"That can't be true." I didn't want to believe that Percy was a killer, but the more evidence I found seemed to compound that theory. Percy didn't have an alibi the day Vanessa died. Someone had left a tarot card regarding her struggle between two men, and Percy had practiced it faithfully. Then there's the diary entry which stated that he'd kill her if she left. Perhaps the stories I'd heard about people confessing to horrendous acts in their final hours were false. Had Percy told me lies as he lay dying?

My phone buzzed in my pocket, and I dropped the Bible back onto the bed. I figured it must be Greg wondering when I'd be home. Instead, I saw Marcia's number pop up on the screen. "My favorite attorney. What's up?"

"Hey." Her voice sounded excited. "Your theory was correct. As it turns out, Patrick did represent Diane Brenner in her divorce proceedings. Like you mentioned, the divorce never happened. At the very last minute, it was called off. Patrick said that they decided to work through their differences."

"Really?" I raised my eyebrows at Jacques, who in turn watched me with curiosity. "Is Patrick at liberty to reveal why they were getting divorced?"

She hesitated. "I'm probably telling you more than I should already."

"Sorry, Marcia. Forget I asked."

Marcia sighed. "Let's just say this. Maybe you want to think about certain celebrity couples, like Brad Pitt and Jennifer Aniston's divorce, or Tiger Woods', perhaps? I think you get the picture now."

"I knew the creep was cheating on her."

Marcia cleared her throat loudly. "Well, it seems that Tom may not have been the only one cheating. He made his own accusations after Diane filed and said she was sleeping with someone too, although Diane denied it. Then all of a sudden, she called Patrick late one night, sobbing into the phone. She said that she still loved Tom and wanted to give him another chance."

Interesting. So Diane may not have been innocent either. However, I still thought she should have run from that psycho while she had the chance. "You don't happen to know when this all went down, do you?"

"I did some snooping myself. It was August 1997," Marcia said. "Two weeks after Percy started serving his sentence."

I sucked in a deep breath. "That's a strange coincidence. What do you think it all means?"

"Maybe nothing," Marcia replied. "Patrick did tell me that the entire family was an emotional train wreck while the trial was going on. They didn't handle anything well—the media, each other, interaction with friends or co-workers. It all could have been due to stress. I mean, first a family member is murdered, and then her husband is found guilty of the crime." She paused. "But I do agree that the timing is weird. Listen, girl, I've got to run. Please don't mention this to anyone."

"You have my word. I appreciate it, Marcia. Lunch is on me next time."

She laughed. "Don't worry about lunch. Sell that house and get me a new client. My business is slow too!"

I disconnected and told Jacques what Marcia had relayed. "Tom and Diane called off the divorce right after Percy went to prison."

He glanced at me sharply. "What do you make of it?"

"Beats me, but it seems that Diane is not an innocent bystander like we originally thought."

"Look," Jacques said. "Stella suffered from dementia for over 20 years, before Percy went to jail. She had money and lots of it. Maybe she decided to leave Diane and Tom a share at the last minute."

"That's possible," I conceded. "Hey, I wonder who took care of Stella when she got sick. Eleanor lived too far away to help out all the time."

"She must have had a nurse," Jacques said.

"Yes, but a member of the family may have been coming to see her regularly too. There must have been someone—like Diane—who checked in on her. They might have had an ulterior motive—to ensure they'd get a slice of the pie."

Jacques glanced at his watch. "We'd better get downstairs."

The Bible tumbled out of my hands and to the floor, and I reached down to grab it. "Let me put this back where I found it. I'm sure Eleanor would love to know that I was snooping through Stella's bedroom instead of the attic."

Jacques snorted. "Yeah, we got a little confused with the locations. Hey, what's wrong?"

I didn't answer. Upon opening the Bible, I discovered that the pages on the right-hand side had been hollowed out. A small wooden box was tucked away inside the book. "Oh wow." I held it out so that Jacques could see.

Jacques took the Bible from my hands after I lifted the box out from within. "Does that have what I think it does inside?"

My hands trembled as I opened the box and removed a white satin pouch which contained something rectangular in shape. "Quite possibly." I opened the pouch and saw that our hunch was correct. An old, fragile set of tarot cards had been tucked inside. I handed them to Jacques. "Should we have Yvette look at these?"

He ran a finger along the edges of the cards. "I guess, but they look like any other deck, except that they're older. Maybe it was Stella's personal deck. What could she have been trying to tell people?"

"The answer is with the cards." I ran my thumb around the wooden box that had been inside the Bible. It was crudely built, as if made by a child, and I wondered if perhaps Percy or Andrew might have made this for their grandmother as a gift. There was a deep groove in one of the corners. Holding my breath, I worked my finger underneath it, and a small section of the wood came loose. There was a lined piece of paper inside.

"Holy confession, Batman," Jacques whispered.

With shaking fingers, I opened the yellowed piece of paper. This must have been what Stella meant. The answer—or the note—was with the cards, not *in* the cards. The writing was cramped cursive and extremely difficult to read. I squinted at the page, barely making out the words. Jacques leaned over my shoulder as I read the note out loud:

My love,

I will never believe that it's over. We belong together. Who cares what anyone else thinks of us? Tomorrow we'll talk, and I'm positive you'll see things from my point of view. Please know that I love you more than anything. I can't live without you and know you feel the same.

There was no signature, but the note was dated September 5, 1996.

"This is dated the day before Vanessa died," I whispered. "It must be from her killer."

CHAPTER EIGHTEEN

Before Jacques and I could say anything further, we heard the front door slam. "Hello? Cindy?"

Eleanor. In a panic I shoved the cards back inside the pouch and deposited it inside my purse, which I had brought upstairs with me. Thankfully I'd brought a mammoth-sized one, and the Bible fit as well.

We had reached the hallway when we heard footsteps on the stairs. Eleanor was already on her way up. The smile I had managed to plaster on my face faded when I saw that she was not alone. Diane was by her side.

"Crap," Jacques muttered under his breath.

They both stared at us, surprised, and then Eleanor smiled warmly. "There you two are. Were you up in the attic? I thought you'd finished sorting all that stuff the other day."

"Yes, we—" At a loss for words, I glanced at Jacques.

"It's all been taken care of Eleanor," he assured her. "One of the attendees at the open house thought that they dropped their cell phone up here, so Cindy and I have been searching the house but to no avail. If you see it, will you please let one of us know?"

Damn, he was good. I had to learn to lie better.

"Certainly." Eleanor glanced from Jacques to me nervously. "I'm glad that I found you two together. There's something I want to tell you both." She hesitated for a moment then glanced over at Diane, who gave me what I thought was a defiant stare in return. "I'd like for Diane and Tom to live in the house until it sells."

Although not in favor of her decision, it wasn't my place to say so. "It's your house, Eleanor. You can certainly do as you please."

Jacques nodded, looking cool and collected about the entire situation. "You're calling the shots, Eleanor." His eyes met mine, and I knew what he was thinking. Jacques wanted me to tell her about what Tom had done earlier.

"The house could sell in no time," I put in. "It's difficult to say. Did you want to take it off the market for a while?" Sadly, the story of my life. Every time I landed a potential good deal, it capsized faster than the Titanic.

Eleanor's tone became agitated. "I'm leaving for California tomorrow. I'm sick of being caught in the middle of all this drama. Tom and Diane need to vacate their house as soon as possible, so this seemed like a good temporary solution for them. Who knows, maybe the house won't sell for another year."

"Would you like us to draw up a contract for a rental?" I asked.

Annoyance crept into Eleanor's face, and she stiffened. "Of course not. I won't charge them to stay here. They're going through some difficult times right now and—"

Diane sniffed. "Eleanor, I'd rather not get into this with strangers."

"You're right, dear. I'm sorry."

Even though I knew the answer to this question, I wanted to gauge Diane's reaction. "How come your grandmother didn't leave the house to you and Tom?"

She seemed startled by my comment. "That's none of your business." She started to go down the stairs, but I reached the top of the landing first and blocked her path. "There's something you should know. Your husband accosted me earlier."

A loud, deafening silence emanated through the room. Then Diane started to laugh. "You're making that up."

"Why would I do that?" I asked in surprise.

She pressed her trembling lips together. "Because you think he killed Percy. He told me so."

Eleanor placed a hand on the railing to steady herself. "Did he strike you?"

I kept my eyes glued on Diane while I answered the question. "No. He'd been drinking and pushed me up against the door and held me there until Jacques found us."

Diane's mouth tightened, and she averted her eyes. "What did you say to set him off?"

Typical. I should have known she'd blame me instead of her husband. The woman was completely delusional. No way would I reveal that my lie about knowing the killer's identity had set Tom off. I couldn't be positive he was the guilty party, but Tom wasn't making a very good case for himself. If I hinted to Eleanor and Diane that I knew who the killer was, they'd start circling me like a pack of hungry wolves, demanding the truth.

I decided to try another tactic. "I asked Tom if he was having an affair with Vanessa."

The color drained from Diane's face. "How dare you," she whispered. "Who the hell do you think you are? You're only a lowlife real estate agent trying to make a fast buck off Eleanor."

This was an accusation I'd heard several times before, but it still always hurt. I pressed my lips together and kept quiet.

Jacques, who'd been watching the entire scene play out, stepped forward. "Mrs. Brenner, your husband exhibited violent behavior toward Cindy. God knows what he might have done to her if I hadn't arrived in time."

I knew I was pushing the envelope but continued. "Why didn't you divorce Tom years ago when you had the chance? Why did you call it off at the last minute?"

Diane's eyes practically bugged out of her head as she looked from me to Eleanor. "How could you?"

"No, I never said a word, Diane," Eleanor insisted.

"It's obvious there's no one I can trust anymore. Maybe there never has been. Mom and Dad never gave a damn about me. Tom and Vanessa did, and I thought you too, but it looks like I was wrong."

"Weren't you the one to find Vanessa's body?" I interrupted, going for the jugular now. "You were supposed to go shopping together the day she died. I heard you were close with your sister-in-law." If Diane had found out that Tom was having an affair with Vanessa, could that have made her snap?

Diane's blue eyes resembled cold, hard steel as they shifted from Eleanor to me. "You're sick to say such a thing. I loved Vanessa and never would have harmed her. Neither did Tom. For the record, you don't know anything about me or my husband. He's been out of work for a while and very depressed. He happens to love *me*." There was a catch in her throat. "I guess he's the only one who ever did." With a sob, she ran down the stairs.

"Diane, don't leave like this!" Eleanor pleaded. She started down the stairs after her and suddenly grabbed the rail with both hands, as if on the verge of a collapse. Jacques and I hurried over and took hold of both of her arms in an attempt to support her.

"Are you okay?" I asked.

Eleanor nodded. Her face was pale, and she was breathing heavily. "I need a minute." She took a step forward while Jacques and I kept hold of her arms.

"Why don't we go down to the kitchen for a cup of tea," I suggested.

She nodded as we slowly descended the stairs. Her breathing was so fast and intense that it frightened me. "Should I call 9-1-1?" I asked.

"No," she whispered. "I have a heart condition. I'm not supposed to get upset."

"Looks like you came to the wrong house for that," Jacques muttered under his breath.

We finally reached the kitchen, and Jacques gently sat her down at the table while I filled the silver kettle sitting on the stove. After rummaging through a few cabinets, I located tea bags and placed one in a cup for her. "Want one?" I asked Jacques.

He shook his head and made a face. Jacques was a coffee man, through and through.

After the water had boiled, I placed the cup in front of Eleanor. She uttered a feeble thank you and took a small sip.

"I want to apologize for Tom's behavior toward you. For the record, Diane wasn't lying. He hasn't worked in a while and been very upset about it." Eleanor blew out a sigh.

"You have nothing to apologize for."

She wrapped her arms around her middle, as if for warmth. "Tom can't even stand to look at me, and it's all because of this damn house. I almost wish that Stella hadn't left it to me. If I didn't need the money, I'd run for the hills."

"It's obvious he has a drinking problem," Jacques said. "How long has that been going on?"

Eleanor ran her hand over the pink and white checkered cloth placemat on the table's surface. "A few years. It's sad to say, but no one has ever liked the man, except for his wife. Tom's always been resentful of those who have more than him. I adore Diane and hoped she'd find happiness with him, but had my doubts from the beginning. I've always had a soft spot for her. You see, she was adopted, and not exactly by choice. Her biological parents were a couple that Mary and Fred—Percy and

Andrew's parents—knew well. They both died in a car accident when Diane was three years old. In their will they'd named Mary and Fred as guardians, in case anything ever happened to them."

"Well, that must have been a surprise," I said.

"Oh, my yes." Eleanor clucked her tongue against the roof of her mouth in apparent disdain. "Mary and Fred weren't cut out to be parents. Every summer they deposited the kids with Stella while they'd travel across Europe like a bunch of adolescent groupies. Stella didn't seem to mind though. She liked having the kids around."

"Fred and Mary didn't have money of their own?" I asked.

She shook her head. "Stella had all the dough and ruled over it with an iron fist. Her husband Simon made a fortune from flipping houses. Back then, there weren't as many people in the business. The man was a master carpenter, and there was nothing he couldn't fix. He started investing money at a very young age and tripled his wealth in a matter of years."

Eleanor paused to catch her breath. "If you wanted money from Stella, it always came at a price. Even though she was fond of Diane, the boys always held her favor. I suspect it's because Diane wasn't a biological heir. Stella could be quite narrow-minded about things like that, and I felt sorry for the girl. You see, I spent a few years in an orphanage myself while growing up and am grateful that didn't happen to Diane. She needed someone to give her attention, and God knows she wasn't getting any from her adoptive parents."

Percy's family gave new meaning to the word dysfunctional. What else had Stella been so narrow-minded about?

Eleanor paused for another sip of tea. "Diane couldn't wait to get out from under her parents' thumbs. She met Tom right after her high school graduation. He was good looking, had a full-time job in a bank, and was always complimenting her on her looks, brain, whatever came to mind. She was so starved for attention that she ate it right up and married him three months after they'd started dating. Mary and Fred were furious, and so was Stella. Stella paid for the wedding but she complained about it for years afterward."

"I'll bet," Jacques murmured.

"A year after Diane's marriage, Fred died of a sudden heart attack. Then Vanessa was killed, and Mary passed on from cancer shortly afterward. Stella was always convinced that Tom had married Diane to get his hands on the family money. She vowed it would never happen, so right before Vanessa died, she announced to the whole family that she was cutting the couple out of her will."

"Jeez," I said in disbelief. "At least you'd think she would have done it privately." Did Stella know that Tom and Diane were both unfaithful to their spouses, and was that another reason why she'd shunned the couple? Plus, why did Andrew not receive anything from his grandmother? Had he lied to me earlier? Someone had, that was for sure. "Did Brenda know Vanessa?" I blurted out suddenly.

Eleanor shot me a strange look. "Andrew and Brenda didn't start dating until several years after Vanessa's death. In answer to your question, Vanessa's younger sister Jennifer and Brenda went to high school together and were on friendly terms, so yes, I believe they knew of each other. Why do you ask?"

What could have been Brenda's motive for wanting Vanessa dead, though? Were they involved with each other? It looked like I would have to get in touch with Jennifer again, this time by phone if she was willing. "Oh, I was only curious."

"Ah, Stella." Eleanor smiled fondly as she thought about her friend. "She was such a character. Large and in charge about everything. Tom almost went nuts when he heard they weren't receiving anything. He and Diane had other problems as well. Before I knew it, they were talking divorce." There was a question in her eyes as she looked at me. "I still don't understand how you would have known about that."

Me and my big mouth. I didn't want to get Marcia or Patrick in trouble, so a little white lie seemed to be in order. "I read about it in one of the articles during Percy's trial."

"Damn reporters," she said bitterly. "They made everyone's life hell when Percy went to prison. The divorce wasn't about Stella's money, though. Tom was fooling around on Diane."

I tried to keep my expression blank. "Do you know who the woman was?"

Eleanor seemed to guess my thoughts. "I don't know who it was, but I can tell you who it definitely *wasn't*. Not Vanessa."

"Are you sure about that?" Jacques inquired.

"Absolutely." Her tone was veiled, and I had my suspicions that she wasn't telling us the truth.

I leaned forward across the table eagerly. "You said before that you thought Stella knew who killed Vanessa. She never gave any clue as to who it was?"

"With her illness, it was difficult to know if she was telling the truth sometimes," Eleanor admitted. "She'd laugh and say something like, 'the answer's in the cards.'"

I raised an eyebrow. "You mean *with* the cards, right?" Was it possible Eleanor knew about the cards upstairs and the note I had found?

Her face grew pensive as she nodded. "It's strange how she always worded it that way, isn't it? But yes, you're right. I do remember her saying that a few times. The answer is *with* the cards." She sighed heavily. "Stella got things confused all the time."

"You were aware that the house would go to you if something happened to Percy, correct? Stella made you executor of her will, so you must have known."

Eleanor acted as if I'd struck her. "How dare you say such a thing," she huffed. "I loved Percy and would never have done anything to hurt him."

I raised a hand in protest. "That isn't what I meant." The last thing I needed now was to alienate her. "It struck me as kind of odd that the house went to you instead of the remaining grandchildren. Please don't take this the wrong way, but what if you had passed on as well? Who would have inherited the house then?"

She shrugged her skinny shoulders. "Naturally, I knew beforehand that the house would go to me—in the event of Percy's death. There weren't any other provisions made. I guess the house would have gone to whoever I chose to leave it to."

Jacques and I were silent. The words were on the edge of my tongue, begging to be said, but lacking sensitivity. I was quickly running out of tact today.

Eleanor's hand shook as she returned her cup to the saucer. "Since you won't ask, I'll tell you. I had a will made out several years ago. I have no family to speak of, so I stated that all of my worldly possessions were to go to Diane."

I knew it. The woman may have written herself a death wish. "Does Diane—do they—I mean—"

"Yes. I've told Diane and am certain Tom knows as well." She rose to her feet. "If you'll both excuse me, I'm going to lie down for a while."

Jacques stood as well. "Do you need some help getting up the stairs?"

"No, thank you. I'm feeling much better now. You can both let yourselves out."

We walked out of the kitchen behind her, through the formal dining room, and into the foyer. Jacques and I watched as she started to climb the stairs and then stopped to turn and stare at both of us. The look in her eyes was of resignation, someone tired of fighting a certain battle. "My flight leaves for California tomorrow at three in the afternoon."

"Safe travels," Jacques murmured. "We'll keep you updated on the status of the house."

"One more thing," I said. "Do you think Stella ever told Percy that she knew who had killed Vanessa?"

She paused, her slender fingers gripping the railing so tight that her knuckles turned white. "I've thought about that many times. For some reason, no, I don't. Percy could be hotheaded at times, and he would have confronted this person the day he got out of jail. I do wonder if she might have left him a clue as to where to find the answer. The last time we spoke was a couple of days before his death. He sounded different from before—distracted and edgy. He said something about confronting one's demons. Then he acted very strange and told me he didn't think he'd be around much longer. When he was on trial, he told Stella, 'Once I know who did this to my wife, I can die peacefully. But not until then.'"

The hairs rose on the back of my neck. If one thing was for certain, Percy had not died peacefully.

Eleanor's voice was feeble as she continued. "The jury thought it was a bunch of bull to make them believe his innocence, but I have no doubt Percy meant what he said."

How had Stella wound up with the note in the first place? If she'd known who the killer was all along, why hadn't she said anything? Had her illness prevented her from doing so?

Eleanor looked as if she was trying to jump inside my brain and discover what I was thinking. "I told you before that I didn't want to be here and am tired of being involved in all this family drama. That much is true. But there's another reason why I want to leave."

I winced inwardly, guessing what she was about to say. "What's that?"

Her dark eyes filled with dread. "I'm worried that I'm next."

CHAPTER NINETEEN

My dreams were anything but dull that night and ranged from the Danson sisters and Sherlock proudly holding up a *Sold* sign to one with Percy lying on the floor, bleeding profusely. He stared up at me and mouthed the words *I didn't do it.* Somewhere in the background, Tom's voice hovered above all as he slurred the words, "You're a liar," over and over at me until I was ready to scream.

In desperation, I covered my ears. "Go away!"

Someone was shaking my arm. "Don't touch me!" I bolted upright in bed, trying to catch my breath.

"Hey." Greg was leaning over me, hand on my arm, his expression concerned. "Are you all right, sweetheart?"

My heart hammered away inside my chest, and I was drenched in sweat. "Yes. It was only a bad dream." Sunshine was streaming through the slits in our window blinds. "What time is it?"

"Almost ten o'clock." He pushed my hair back from my face and kissed me tenderly.

"Oh my God." I started to get out of bed, but he stopped me. "You shouldn't have let me sleep this late."

"It's Sunday," Greg said. "My mother's downstairs with the kids, and you needed the rest. Now tell me about your dream. That bastard who manhandled you yesterday was in it—I know he was."

"No," I lied. After I'd told Greg what had happened last night, it had taken considerable pleading and effort on my part to keep him from leaving the house when he insisted he was about to go "rearrange the guy's face." Never mind the fact that he didn't know where Tom lived.

A muscle ticked in Greg's jaw. "I won't have anyone treating my wife like that. Someone needs to beat the crap out of him, and I'm up for the job."

"But Jacques could get into trouble, and I don't want to take that chance," I protested. "He's dealing with enough right now. Tom only scared me—he didn't hurt me."

Greg rolled his eyes in irritation. "If that's what you really want, I'll go along with it, but for the record, I'm not happy about it. Now tell me what else is bothering you, and don't say nothing, because that's a lie."

Wearily, I leaned back against the pillows. "I'm worried about Eleanor. She isn't safe while she's still in that house. Somebody wants that mansion—or something inside—bad enough to kill for it. *Again*."

Greg's blue eyes widened. "Do you think they're searching for the note that you and Jacques found?"

"There's a good chance," I admitted. "Maybe the killer doesn't know exactly what the item is, but they know there's something that could condemn them. They may even have looked for it themselves at some point. Or Stella blabbed about it and then didn't remember doing so."

He gently caressed my cheek. "That woman sounds like she was quite the force to be reckoned with."

"Definitely not your typical sweet old lady." I drew a sharp breath. "The sale isn't even important to me anymore. I'd like to get justice for Percy but don't want to spend any more time away from the baby and the kids."

Greg gave me that sexy lopsided grin of his. "Kids? What about me? I haven't gotten much attention lately."

I kissed him. "You've been spoiled for years."

"True." He nuzzled my neck. "Listen, if you'd rather not go back to the house, baby, then don't. Jacques can take care of everything. You shouldn't be doing all this so soon after the baby's birth anyway. I don't want you to get sick."

I glanced over at the crib. "Where *is* the baby?"

"Downstairs with my mother. I just gave her a bottle. Darcy's in the shower, and the twins are watching television. There's breakfast waiting for you whenever you feel like it. Mom made pancakes."

I reached for my robe at the edge of the bed. "Did she lace mine with cyanide?"

"No, she's fresh out," he teased. "And I'm cooking dinner tonight, so no worries of poison there."

I wrapped both of my arms around his waist as we went downstairs together. "You're too good to me."

"It's all part of my job." He kissed me on the top of my head. "Now, we have to talk about Valentine's Day. What do you want to do?"

We went into the empty kitchen, and I fixed myself a cup of caffeine-free herbal tea. "No idea." Dressing up and going out seemed like too much of an effort right now.

My phone vibrated from the kitchen counter where I'd left it last night, and I glanced down at the screen. "It's Jacques," I said to Greg before picking up. "Hey, boss."

"Hey yourself, little mama," Jacques replied. He sounded more like his old relaxed self today. "Look, I know this is last minute, but the office just received notification that someone wants to see 25 Rodgers Way in an hour. They asked for you specifically."

Cripes. There was no getting away from this house. "No can do. I need to spend the day with my family. If you have to get Stacey to show it, I understand."

"Stacey's out of town today." He sighed heavily. "I'll go. Ed can wait a little while."

"Hold on a second. What do you mean? Are you guys getting back together?" I held my breath in anticipation.

"We were supposed to meet for lunch at noon, but no worries. I can be a little late."

Guilt overwhelmed me. "No, I don't want you to do that. I'll be there."

"Forget it. I promised to take care of the showings, and you did the open house yesterday. I wouldn't have even asked except that the customer requested you by name, so I figured they knew you personally."

My curiosity peaked. "Woman or man?"

There was a pause. "A husband and wife by the name of Johnson. Zoe said the guy's first name was Bernie."

The name was not familiar. Had I shown them a house before? Maybe they had a home to sell as well and needed an agent. *Aargh.* I hated to pass this opportunity up. "Well, if you're sure."

"Positive. I'll let you know how it goes. Have a good day, darling." He clicked off without another word.

I stood there, lost in thought for a moment. Jacques had done so much for me, and I couldn't even handle this one little favor for him in return. His business and his personal life were both hanging by a thread, yet he never complained. Some friend I was.

Greg poured himself a cup of coffee. "What's wrong, baby?"

"Would you mind if I left for an hour to show Percy's—err, Eleanor's house?"

A frown creased his handsome face. "You just told me you wanted to take a step back, Cin."

I pressed the button for Jacques' number. "I know, but a client asked for me specifically, and Jacques was going to meet Ed for lunch. They need to get back together."

"You've got a heart of gold." He came over and kissed me. "If you feel that strongly about it, go ahead. But please be careful and don't overdo."

"Thank you," I managed to say before Jacques' voicemail message finished playing. "Jacques, it's me. I'll take the showing. You go meet Ed and have a great time. I'll text you when it's over."

The door to the den flew open, and Helen came out with Grace in her arms. "So, you're off gallivanting again, I see."

My eye started to twitch. "Helen, there's no need for you to put yourself out. Greg can take care of the baby."

Greg held out his hands for Grace. "Mom, I have done this a few times before, remember."

Helen narrowed her eyes and addressed Greg as she handed him the baby. "I think it's disgusting that your wife—a new mother, for crying out loud—can't even stay home with her baby. She's always traipsing off somewhere." She continued to stare at Greg with pity. "You could have done so much better, son."

The twins appeared behind her in the doorway with Rusty stationed between them. "What does traipsing mean?" Stevie asked.

Greg's face reddened. "Don't speak that way to my wife, Mom. Especially with the kids around."

"Grandma was telling us all about the other girls you could have married," Seth chimed in. "She's not sure why you picked Mom."

"Shush!" Helen said angrily.

I pointed toward the stairs in the living room. "Guys, get upstairs to your room."

They stood there motionless, staring at me.

"Now!"

Seth led the way out of the kitchen while Stevie followed, grumbling. "Every time they don't want you to hear something fun, you have to go to your room."

"Yeah," Seth agreed. "How are we ever supposed to learn anything?"

Greg waited until he heard them jogging up the stairs and turned back to his mother. "You wanted to come here, Mom. We appreciate everything you've done, but I won't have you talking to Cindy like that."

"Helen." I chose my words very carefully. "If you have a problem with me, let's discuss it between ourselves and *not* in front of the kids."

She sniffed out loud. "You keep saying you want to be home with your kids, but every time I see you, you're running off, *supposedly* to show a house. Let's face it. We all know you can't make a sale if your life depended on it, so what are you *really* doing?"

"Mom!" Greg's nostrils flared in anger. "Stop this now!"

I'd finally had enough. For years this woman had managed to intimidate me, and I'd tried in vain to keep the peace, but no more. I squared my shoulders and put my face up against hers. She backed up against the kitchen counter and started to squirm with discomfort. *Good.* First part of mission accomplished.

"What am I really doing?" I repeated in a sarcastic tone. "I must be off with the UPS guy, since he's really Grace's father. Or maybe the mailman. No, wait. I'm having an affair with the paper boy. There are so many different options for me to choose from."

Greg's mouth twitched at the corners, but he said nothing. Helen stood there, arms folded across her chest, and lifted her icy eyes to meet mine.

"This is *my* house, Helen. I'm grateful for your help with the baby and the kids, but I think it's time for you to go to a hotel now. If you need money, we'll give you some."

I glanced over at Greg, unsure of what his reaction might be. His mother had been a touchy subject since day one. Greg was her only son, and he'd turned out to be such a compassionate human being with this reptile as a parent.

Helen jutted out her chin in defiance and looked over at Greg. "Are you going to let your wife talk to me like this?" she demanded. "Your *own* mother?"

Greg's expression was sympathetic. "I'm afraid you've had this coming for a long time, Mom. I love you, but Cindy and the kids have to come first."

Helen bit into her lower lip and moved away from me. "Fine. I'll leave right away. I guess I know when I'm not wanted." She stepped back into the den and slammed the door behind her.

Greg and I both heaved a sigh in unison. Mine was of relief, but his may well have been of regret. He was rocking Grace, who had mercifully slept through all the drama. I crossed the room to stand next to him and kissed his cheek. "Thank you for standing up for me."

He gave me a sober smile. "It was way overdue. I should have stopped her long ago, Cin. Frankly I don't know what her problem is."

That she can't stand me and never will. "I need to run upstairs and grab a shower. If I hurry, I'll barely make it in time. There's a bottle of breast milk in the fridge for the baby."

A wide grin spread across his face. "If you really want to thank me, you'll let me take my beautiful wife out on the town for Valentine's Day. Start thinking about where you'd like to go."

I turned around in the doorway. "But that's impossible."

His face creased in a frown. "Why?"

"We no longer have a babysitter," I teased and blew him a kiss.

I hurried up the stairs and jumped into the shower. Fifteen

minutes later I dried my hair and dressed in black wool slacks and a beige sweater. I stuffed my feet into a pair of boots and grabbed my car keys. On my way downstairs I met Greg coming up. He was putting Grace to bed and I kissed both of them. "I shouldn't be more than an hour."

"We'll be here. Drive safe, baby."

I grabbed my briefcase from the kitchen counter and hurried out the front door. The traffic was heavy for a Sunday, and I arrived at Eleanor's five minutes late. Then I noticed Jacques' car in the driveway. Shoot. I had hoped to save him the trip. Well, maybe it still wasn't too late. My fingers flew as I typed out a text to him. *I left you a voicemail to tell you I'd take the showing. Why don't I come in and you can take off to meet Ed?*

I waited for a minute with the engine running until my phone pinged with a return message from Jacques. *Yes. Come in.*

I grabbed my briefcase and got out of the car. Too late, I realized I hadn't latched it properly. Papers spilled out onto the driveway, and I cursed under my breath. As I gathered them up in a hurry, my eyes fell upon the open house sign-in sheet from yesterday.

Absently I glanced at the names as I put the sheet back into my briefcase. *Gina and Rob Swisher*. We hadn't received feedback yet, but it had only been a day. *Gloria and Lila Danson.* Yeah, in my worst nightmare.

That was when I noticed the names underneath the Danson sisters for the first time. It struck me as odd that all of the Rodgers clan had signed the sheet. Was this an attempt to mock me? Tom had even written "my house" in parentheses next to his name. What a jerk. Even Diane had signed when she stopped with Eleanor. Weird. I looked at all the signatures again, and then my heart gave a little stutter. One of the signatures looked very familiar.

No. It can't be.

The pouch with the note and the Bible we'd found were still

in my purse. With trembling fingers, I placed the note from Vanessa's admirer alongside the open house sheet.

One of the signatures was a perfect match.

"Oh God," I whimpered low in my throat. Blood roared in my ears as I put the note back into the pouch and then inside the Bible. I left it on the back seat and shut my car door, the sound echoing in my head. I snapped my briefcase shut and even took extra care to make sure it was latched this time.

My stomach rumbled with dread. I was certain I knew who had killed Vanessa and probably Percy as well. Despite the cold I stood by the side of the car and shot off another text to Jacques. *You need to get rid of these people ASAP. I know who the killer is.*

I waited another minute, shivering in the chilly winter air. There was no response this time. Resigned, I went to the front door. Somehow, I'd have to get Jacques away from the clients for a minute so that we could talk privately. The front door was unlocked. I opened it and left my briefcase on the small table in the foyer. "Hello?" I called out.

The house was eerily silent, and a slight chill moved down my back, as if a premonition of sorts. "Jacques?"

"In the great room, Cindy." His voice was faint, as if he was talking within a bubble. Puzzled, I entered the room and immediately froze.

Jacques was lying on the floor in a fetal position. His face was bloody and bruised, his glasses lying broken next to him. I couldn't even tell where the blood was coming from. My hands flew to my face in horror as I stifled a sob.

There was a man standing next to him in an immaculate navy suit, pressed to perfection. The one person I did not want to see right now. My hunch had been correct, but that was of little comfort to me. He moved the gun away from Jacques' head and pointed it directly at me.

"Hello, Cindy," Andrew greeted me cordially. "I was hoping you'd show up."

CHAPTER TWENTY

A scream escaped from my lips. "What did you do to him?" I started to rush toward Jacques, but Andrew clicked the hammer on the gun and I froze in my tracks.

"Take it easy there, Jessica Fletcher wannabe," he warned. "Don't try to be a hero. Your little friend is fine. When he saw the gun, he foolishly tried to wrestle it away from me. Lucky for him I didn't kill him. He took a couple of blows to the head and blacked out for a few minutes. While he was out cold, I responded to your texts."

"Let her go," Jacques moaned. His green eyes were dull and vacant as they stared up at Andrew helplessly. "She has kids who need her. Do what you want with me instead."

Andrew grinned at me. "You sure you're not sleeping with this guy? He's regular knight in shining armor material."

This couldn't be happening to us. Yes, I'd already figured out that Andrew had killed Vanessa. The handwriting from the note and his signature on the open house form were a perfect match. When Jacques and I first saw the illegible cursive, we should have realized that it was a doctor's scrawl. The writing had barely been legible. As a dentist, Andrew fit the profile perfectly.

Suddenly it was all clear. Andrew had been the one having the affair with Vanessa, not Tom as I'd originally thought. Like a jigsaw puzzle, the pieces all fit together now.

"You killed Vanessa because she wouldn't leave Percy for you," I accused him. "Then you killed Percy because he managed to figure it out."

He narrowed his eyes and pointed the gun at me again. "How did you know about Vanessa refusing to leave Percy? Does that old bird Eleanor know it too?"

I shook my head. "There was an entry in Vanessa's diary that said, 'he'll kill me if I leave.' We originally thought it was about Percy." It had, in fact, referred to Andrew. Vanessa must have realized at some point in their relationship that he was unbalanced.

Yvette's interpretation from the tarot cards came back to haunt me again. *You and a person you love will be in a bad situation very soon. Someone may die.* The odds were definitely against both Jacques and me, and we needed the precious commodity of time. There had to be a way out. "How did Percy know you killed Vanessa? Did Stella tell him?"

Andrew leaned back against the desk—the same desk where I'd found Percy's body—the gun never wavering in his hands. A faraway look came into his eyes. "God, she was so beautiful. The first time Percy introduced me to her and said they were going to be married, I wanted her. She got bored with him quick—I knew he wasn't her type. She was daring, wild, and loved to party. He was the type that wanted a candlelight dinner and toasty fireplace. What a dud." His face filled with contempt.

"He was your brother," I said with disbelief. "How could you take his life?"

"That woman occupied my every waking hour, every thought and dream. She consumed me." A hungry look came into his eyes. "We were great together. Every Tuesday and

Thursday we'd meet up at a local hotel. I desired Vanessa like a drug addict craves crack. I couldn't get enough of her."

Jacques was breathing heavily from his curled-up position on the floor. I slowly knelt beside him, keeping my eyes on Andrew the entire time. He watched but made no attempt to stop me.

"Hang in there." I cradled Jacques' head between my hands. "You're going to be okay."

"No," Jacques said faintly. "Not this time, Cin."

Tears welled in the corners of my eyes. There had to be a way out of this. *Think, think.*

Andrew ignored our heartfelt exchange. "My stupid brother finally got wind that something was going on behind his back, but he didn't know who his wife was sleeping with. Percy may have loved her too, but not as much as I did."

"You loved her so much that you killed her." My tone was flippant and full of sarcasm. *Sick bastard.*

Again, it was as if Andrew was in some type of trance and couldn't hear me. "Percy told her that if she didn't break it off with the other guy, he wanted a divorce." He shook his head forlornly. "Never in a million years did I think that she'd stay with him. One afternoon when Percy was off on some errand, I went over to their house to confront Vanessa. She told me that there was no changing her mind. She'd decided to end our affair and was staying with Percy. She said—" Andrew laughed bitterly. "She said something like, 'I think you should go for a psychological evaluation.' Sure thing. No slut is ever going to tell me that I'm crazy."

Right. Because he was most definitely normal.

"We were in the kitchen," Andrew continued. "I grabbed Vanessa by the arm, and she slapped me and pushed me away. I gave her one last chance to change her mind, but she refused. What a stupid, stupid girl. So I picked up the knife from the counter, and in one quick movement, I sliced her throat." He stared down at the floor, as if he could still see her lifeless body lying there. "She just lay there and didn't move. So. Much. Blood."

Nausea washed over me, and I thought I might be sick. His voice was callous and unfeeling. "How could you kill Vanessa if you loved her?"

His eyes were dark with disdain. "You don't understand. I couldn't bear the thought of her being intimate with Percy again. If I couldn't have her, there was no way in hell I'd let him have her either."

A chill ran down my spine as those ominous eyes continued to stare into mine. Andrew didn't care about me. He didn't care about Jacques. The man wasn't playing with a full deck of tarot cards. "Why leave the card by her body? To make it look like Percy killed her?"

He gave me a smug look. "Of course. He and my grandmother loved to fool around with tarot. I knew the basic meaning of some of the cards but never understood what all the fuss was about. What better way to incriminate him than to leave one at the scene of the crime, right? Plus, it was his house, and he had no alibi. When I killed Percy, I couldn't resist doing it again. Do you think the police made the connection?"

This time I chose to ignore *his* question. "What about your grandmother? How did she know that you'd killed Vanessa?"

Andrew considered this carefully. "After the police were done with the investigation, Gram and my sister went over to Percy's to finish the cleanup. The police swore that they searched the house for any type of clues, but I'm guessing Gram must have found the note I'd written Vanessa. Maybe it was hidden in her diary. I'm not sure. Gram bought it for her—she bought one for all the girls."

When I didn't respond, Andrew smiled and moved the gun from me to Jacques. He was clearly enjoying this—being the center of attention while he continued to terrorize us with the gun. Jacques lay still on the floor. His face was so pale that I was afraid if he didn't get medical attention soon, it might be too late. A small sob escaped from my lips.

Andrew gave me a mocking grin. "I smell fear. Well, you should be afraid. It's the same type of fear Vanessa knew when she crossed me." He tipped his head back and laughed. "Percy was such a schmuck. He made it all so easy for me. The police lifted his fingerprints off the knife that was used, but I wore gloves. A neighbor testified that she saw them arguing earlier that morning. The police took him into custody the same day."

Poor Percy had never stood a chance. I tried to swallow the terror rising in my throat. "Why would Stella keep the note all these years and never tell that you killed Vanessa?" Then the answer hit me. "Wait a second. *You* were her favorite, not Percy."

A flash of raw emotion flickered in his eyes then went out, as if a flame had suddenly been extinguished. "Yeah. She did love me—once. But after Percy went to jail, Gram became rotten to the core. I suspected that she might know, but she never said anything. She also started to get sick about that time, so who knows if she would have come out with the truth eventually? Then came the big blow—when she died and left Percy everything. Gram always told me I'd be her sole heir. It was our little secret."

Andrew scratched the side of his face with the barrel of the gun as he continued. "That BS line of hers, 'the answer is with the cards.' Good thing I placed that bug in her room, or else I never would have heard you two find that deck yesterday." His eyes were an endless cold abyss as he surveyed me with contempt. "You knew it was me—I saw the text you sent your buddy here."

I answered his accusation with one of my own. "Percy never made a pass at your girlfriend. You made that part up."

He smiled. "Correct. But tell me, how did you know where to look for the deck of cards?"

"Just lucky, I guess." It was difficult to know how the old woman's mind had worked. Maybe she had planned to tell and then gotten so sick that she'd forgotten about it. Or perhaps she didn't want to see another grandson—her favorite—go to prison as well.

Andrew seemed to guess my thoughts. "She was a strange old bird. She loved Percy and me more than her own daughter —my mother. She never accepted Diane since she wasn't a biological heir." His face was pensive. "She must have struggled with her demons for a long time." He snapped his fingers, and the crazy man was back again. "Tough break, huh? Now, are you done interrogating me?"

Before I could utter another word, he yanked me roughly to my feet. "Where's the note I wrote Vanessa? You'd better have it with you. I asked for you to come today—not this joker." He nudged Jacques with his foot. "Now because of your stupidity, you both have to die."

Anger rose from the pit of my stomach. "He's no joker. He has more courage in his pinky finger than you have in your entire body."

"Careful," Andrew warned. As if to make a point, he aimed the gun at the ceiling and fired. There was a silencer on it, but the vibration was still enough to terrify me. A piece of Sheetrock flew through the air and broke into several pieces next to the desk.

Andrew flashed me an evil smile. "I have three bullets left. Hey, there's even one for me, but hell, I'm not planning on going anywhere." He laughed. "Now, I asked you, where's the note?"

"Can I ask one more question?" I pleaded. "How did Percy figure it out? What happened when you came here to see him?"

His smile faded. "Ah, dear big brother Percy. He thought he was so clever. My guess is that he found the note too. I assume that Gram may have told him about her infamous 'the answer is with the cards' line at one time. He called me up out of the blue and asked me to stop by the house. Said that he needed my opinion about something. What a crock. He never could stand me, and the feeling was mutual. When I got here, he asked me point-blank if I was the one who had killed Vanessa. I denied it, but then he tipped his hand. 'I saw the note,' he said to me. 'You're going to take responsibility.' Andrew made a *tsk-tsk* sound. "Foolish, foolish Percy."

Andrew's forehead was shining with sweat. He moved the sleeve of his overcoat to wipe his face as he continued. "So I told Percy, 'Hey, let's talk about this for a minute.' But Percy said no, he was turning me in and to get out of his house. He couldn't bear to look at me anymore. Boy, that's rich. I had my switch-blade in my pocket. Percy's back was to me while he dialed the phone and asked for the police. He never finished the call." Andrew shook his head in disbelief. "Didn't he know you should never turn your back on a killer?"

The air was thick and warm, and beads of perspiration trickled down the small of my back. How long had we been here? It seemed like days.

"So, same as Vanessa, I slit his throat. God, that feeling of power was so incredible." He started to laugh and rocked back on his heels and grinned at me. "I placed a kitchen knife in Percy's hand to make it look like a suicide. But I had no idea that you would be dropping by and find him before he was actually dead. You almost ruined everything."

"You're sick." The words fell out of my mouth before I could stop them.

He reached out and grabbed me roughly by the shoulder. "Now, for the last time, where's the note, Miss Fletcher?"

"Don't give it to him." Jacques' voice was barely audible, his breath coming in painful gasps.

Andrew rolled his eyes at Jacques, and then, without further warning, he reached down and whacked him in the head with the gun. Jacques let out a moan and lay still.

"Leave him alone!" I screamed and knelt beside my friend again. I sobbed and held his bleeding head in my hands. "Jacques, say something, please."

"I'm okay," he whispered.

He was definitely *not* okay. There was blood everywhere, and his face was as white as chalk. Tears ran down my cheeks, and he gave me a sad smile. "I love you, Cin. Don't forget that."

"The note," Andrew growled. He gestured at my handbag on the floor. "Is it in there?"

I wiped my eyes with the back of my hand. A plan had started to take shape in the recesses of my brain. "It's outside. In the car."

Andrew yanked me off the ground and placed the gun next to my temple. "If you try to leave, I *will* kill him. Do not doubt that for a second. Then I'll shoot the tires out on your vehicle, and you'll be a goner too. Understand?"

Panic engulfed my entire body, but somehow, I managed to bob my head up and down. "I won't leave. Please don't hurt him again. I'll get the note and come back inside. But it's—you misunderstood. The note's in Jacques' car, not mine. I left it with him yesterday."

A muscle moved in Jacques' jaw, but his face gave away nothing. He must have realized what I was up to. When our eyes met, he simply nodded his head. He knew this was our only chance. "It's locked," he said. "Keys—the keys are in my pocket. Can't reach—"

"For crying out loud," Andrew muttered impatiently. He leaned down, grabbed the key ring from Jacques' coat pocket, and threw it at me. "I'll be standing in the doorway. Don't try anything stupid. Do I make myself clear?"

Once again, I bobbed my head up and down in reply. I slowly moved forward across the room, with Andrew following close behind me. My legs were like Jell-O, their movement uncontrollable and wobbly. I stumbled when I reached the foyer, and Andrew screamed a four-letter expletive. He grabbed me roughly by the arm and threw me against the door. My head connected with the colored pane of glass, and I moaned as pain set in.

Andrew opened the door. "You've got two minutes before I shoot your friend. Now move."

It had started to sleet outside. The wet mixture pelted my face and mixed with my tears. I beeped open Jacques' car and then promptly dropped the keys on the blacktop. As I picked them up, I glanced around. The street was quiet, except for the sounds of the winter mixture hitting the ground. There were no cars or people in sight. No one to help Jacques and me. Andrew watched from the doorway. The house was set far enough back from the road and hidden by the row of evergreen trees that no one would see him.

It was all up to me now. Jacques was hurt too badly to help. I didn't know how much blood he'd lost, but it might be life threatening. Thoughts of Greg, the kids, and my precious new baby flashed through my mind. Yes, they needed me, but I couldn't and wouldn't desert Jacques in his hour of need. I owed the man too much and loved him like a brother. I would not turn my back on him but also knew with certainty that when I returned to the house, Andrew would kill us both.

With shaking hands, I reached under Jacques' seat until I found the item that I was looking for. Then I righted myself and reached over the visor on the driver's side. There was an envelope inside the flap. It was most likely Jacques' insurance cards, but Andrew wouldn't know that. They would work fine for my purpose.

I shut the door of the car and even made sure to lock it. Andrew was watching intently, so I placed the envelope in my right coat pocket and kept my hand inside it as well. My boots crunched on the icy surface as I slowly trudged back up the driveway. A broad smile spread across Andrew's face, and he lowered the gun to his side.

My heart banged against the wall of my chest with every step. As I positioned my fingers inside the pocket, my hand shook ever so slightly.

There was no turning back now. I would not fail my friend.

"Took you long enough," Andrew muttered. He reached out his empty hand for the envelope. "Give it to me."

I withdrew my hand from the coat pocket, raised Jacques' pistol in front of me, closed my eyes, and fired.

CHAPTER TWENTY-ONE

"Okay." Officer Henderson's voice sounded weary. "Once again, what happened after you fired the gun?"

I understood that the man had a job to do, but my patience had started to wear thin. I wanted to see how Jacques was doing. "He fell. Then I called 9-1-1."

The policeman made another note on his pad and then stopped to examine it. Irritation continued to build inside me, and finally I couldn't stand it anymore. "Are we almost done? I'd like to—"

The door of the emergency room pushed open, and Greg hurried in. His expression was sheer panic until he saw us sitting in the corner. He rushed over, ignoring the curious glances of onlookers nearby. "Oh my God, baby. Are you okay?"

I buried my head into his chest and inhaled the scent of him—his musky cologne mixing with the frigid air from outside. "Yes, now that you're here. Jacques will be all right too." When I thought back to how ill he'd looked in the ambulance, tears filled my eyes. "They took him downstairs for a CAT scan a little while ago."

"Does he have any other injuries?" Greg asked.

"I don't know. Jacques needed staples in his head, and he has a concussion. He'll be here for at least one night, maybe more. Ed's with him now. They only want one visitor in there at a time."

Officer Henderson's radio blared through the room, and he rose out of the chair while holding up a finger to us. "Excuse me, folks. I have all that I need for now, Mrs. York. We may have more questions for you later."

Greg watched him walk away and then gazed at me with enormous blue eyes. "Level with me. Did you know this Andrew guy was a killer when you got there? Please don't tell me you went inside the house aware that he was waiting for you."

I bit into my lower lip. "No. I didn't know he was in there with Jacques. Andrew had requested me for the showing because he thought I might have figured out that he was the killer. He put a bug in Stella's room a while back and overheard the exchange between Jacques and me when we found the note yesterday. When I went inside the house, Jacques was lying on the floor, and he was bleeding—" I whimpered out loud and didn't finish the sentence.

Greg's voice was ragged as he wrapped his arms around me. "Don't cry, baby. You're both fine. That's all that matters."

As I rested my head on his shoulder, I saw Ed Kapinski come out of the emergency room door. He was over six feet tall and bald as an eagle with an ethereal air about him. We got along well enough, even though I didn't see him often. While Jacques was a talker, Ed only spoke when he had something meaningful to say. I guess opposites really did attract.

His piercing brown eyes were sober as he walked over to us and shook Greg's hand. To my surprise, he then put his arms around me. Ed wasn't a demonstrative person.

"Jacques would like to see you," he said gruffly. "They're taking him up to a private room shortly, but he wanted you to come back there first. Plus I wanted to say thank you."

The emotion in his voice was enough to set my tear ducts in motion again. I kissed him on the cheek and then turned back to Greg. "I won't be long."

Greg smiled wistfully at me. "Take all the time you need, baby. Ed looks like he could use a cup of coffee. How about we go downstairs to the cafeteria?"

Ed nodded in silence as they walked out of the emergency room together. I bypassed the receptionist and entered the treatment area through the same door that Ed had come out of. I stared at the array of curtains and wished I had asked Ed where Jacques might be.

A nurse walked past me wheeling an EKG machine. "Who are you looking for?"

"Mr. Forte."

She nodded and pointed a finger. "Third curtain on the right."

"Thank you." I peeked around the curtain first and saw him lying in bed, his eyes closed. There was an IV on one side of him and a heart monitor positioned on the other. His face had more color than it had when he was in the ambulance. I tried to keep my voice steady and lighthearted. "Is everyone decent in here?"

He opened his eyes and blinked. "No, but come in anyway."

I sat on the chair next to his bed and reached for his hand. "How do you feel?"

"I've got one mother of a headache. Where's Ed?"

"He went down to the cafeteria with Greg to get some coffee," I replied.

Jacques squeezed my hand tightly. "I never got a chance to say thank you in the ambulance."

"That's okay." I leaned over and kissed his cheek. "You were a little out of it."

"You saved my life," he whispered.

I refused to cry again, especially since Jacques wouldn't want to witness the spectacle. "Well, you've done the same thing for me, so let's just say I was returning the favor."

We sat there in companionable silence for a minute, listening to a nurse talking to a patient in the next curtained-off area. Finally, Jacques spoke. "Andrew. Did he—I mean—" He stopped when he saw my face. "Cin—"

I shut my eyes for a brief second. "Yes, he's dead."

Jacques patted my arm in reassurance. "You did what you had to. He would have killed us both for sure."

I didn't answer. There was nothing I could say to that.

"Have you talked to the police?" he asked.

"Yes, a little while ago. I don't think there will be any repercussions. They seem to believe my claim that it was self-defense."

Jacques continued to watch me with pensive green eyes. "Are you okay?"

"Not a bruise on me," I said cheerfully but knew what he meant. No, I wasn't okay. This would haunt me for the rest of my life. I had killed a man. Yes, it had been necessary to save my best friend and myself, but that didn't make it any easier. Somehow, I'd have to move past this and get on with the rest of my life. But I would never forget.

"You solved a twenty-year-old murder case, Cin," Jacques said. "You got justice for both Percy and his wife. I'm so proud of you."

"Poor Percy," I said wistfully. He was the real victim and deserved all our sympathy. What a tragic waste of a life. I couldn't even fathom what that must have been like for him—to spend 20 years in prison for a crime he didn't commit and then to be murdered himself.

Eleanor had been ready to board her plane when I'd reached her. After I relayed my news, she had cried openly on the phone and canceled her flight. She'd then called Diane, who had gone to the morgue with Brenda to identify Andrew's body. Neither of them or Tom had been in contact with me, and that was fine. Honestly, I hoped to never lay eyes on any of them again.

I decided to change the subject. "Hey, guess what. You're not going to believe this. We have an offer on the house."

Jacques looked at me in disbelief. "You're joking."

"Would I joke about something like that?"

Jacques' eyes gleamed with interest. "Who? And how much?"

"Well, well. Someone's looking better already," I teased. "The couple that came to the open house yesterday is very interested. The Swishers' agent called me while you were downstairs for your CAT scan. Now for the bad news. They want to offer a hundred grand less than the asking price."

Jacques rolled his eyes wearily. "I hate it when people play lowball like that. Did Eleanor say to counter offer?"

I shook my head. "Nope. She flat out agreed to it. She only wanted to know how fast it could be done."

"What?" Jacques sat up in surprise.

"Hey, take it easy." I gently lowered his head back onto the pillow. "Eleanor wants to be rid of the place and all its unpleasant memories. I totally get that. She even talked about giving Diane a share of the profit. Hey, it is Eleanor's house, so that's her prerogative. Let's look on the bright side. It will still be a great commission for the agency."

A smile flickered across his face. "You realize what this means, darling. You've finally gotten that million-dollar deal you've been dying for."

I winced. "Great choice of words there."

"Sorry." He beamed at me. "You did it, girl. Again, I'm so proud of you."

It was difficult to keep the grin off my face. Ever since I'd started selling real estate over four years ago, I'd dreamed of making a big deal. Sometimes it felt like I was the only one in the business who'd never sold a million-dollar house. It was a good feeling but, given everything that had happened, not as good as I'd originally thought it would be.

"I have some news too," Jacques announced. He was looking more like his old self as the conversation wore on, and I said a silent prayer of thanks that we'd both come out of this nightmare alive.

"Oh?" I leaned closer to him. "This wouldn't happen to do with a certain good-looking bald guy I saw in the waiting room, would it?"

His eyes twinkled merrily. "I'm moving back in. Ed apologized. He said that this was a total wakeup call for him, almost losing me like that."

I exhaled a deep breath. "Wow, I'm so happy for you both. That's the best news I've heard all day—even better than the sale."

Jacques held up a hand. "You didn't let me finish. We've also decided to compromise. We're going to adopt a child—an older one, around Stevie and Seth's age. One of Ed's customers is an adoption attorney, and she knows of a seven-year-old boy who's available in China."

The waterworks started again as I reached over to hug him. "You guys will make amazing parents. This is such wonderful news."

"I'm glad you feel that way," Jacques said. "Because I have a favor to ask."

"Anything."

"We'd like to babysit your kids soon," Jacques announced. "You know—to get in a little experience ahead of time."

I raised my eyebrows. "You do know what the twins are capable of, right?"

He tried to frown, but the corners of his mouth turned up slightly and gave him away. "Yes. And regardless, we still want to watch them."

"I CAN'T BELIEVE you're letting those two fruity friends of yours babysit the boys when someone like *me* is available." Helen tossed her head defiantly.

Greg threw up his hands in resignation and looked at me. Helen had come over to the house to collect the rest of her things. Her roof had been completed the same day I'd kicked her out, so she hadn't even needed to go to a hotel. A wonderful coincidence.

It was Valentine's Day, and Darcy was off at a school dance, while Greg and I were going out to dinner. When I'd told Jacques about our plans, he'd asked if he and Ed could come by and spend the evening with the twins and Grace. At first, I'd been concerned since Jacques had only gotten out of the hospital the day before, but he had promised to take it easy. They were bringing Chinese food, ice cream, and DVDs. The twins were looking forward to the evening as much as Ed and Jacques were.

I handed the baby to Greg and managed to force a smile to my lips. "Well Helen, I have to agree—there is no one like you. You're in a class all by yourself."

She gave me a sharp look but said nothing.

"Mom," Greg protested. "Jacques and Ed are good people. Plus, they're adopting a child of their own soon and want to watch the boys. It's nothing personal."

Helen gave a little snort. I knew that Greg was trying to smooth her ruffled feathers over but was sorely tempted to add my own sentiments. *Yes Helen, it is personal. I'd rather have those two dear friends of mine babysit any day of the week instead of a judgmental windbag like you.* But instead I merely smiled and reminded myself that Helen was like a big baby herself at times.

"What are you smiling at, Cynthia?" Helen asked sourly.

"Oh it's nothing really," I assured her. "I'm looking forward to spending a little time with the UPS guy—oops, I mean your son tonight."

Greg started to laugh so hard that I was worried he might drop the baby. I reached over to take her from him.

"Well, I never." Helen's face was crimson as she scanned the room in annoyance. "Where did you move my car keys? I need to get out of this insane asylum."

"They're on the kitchen table." Helen's keys were resting next to the new folders that Jacques had made for the agency. The inspections for Eleanor's house had gone down without a hitch today, and my copy of the test results were inside. Helen glanced absently at the folder then picked it up and studied the cover carefully. A group picture of the entire agency was displayed on the front, which included Jacques, Stacey, Zoe, me, and Ariel before she'd left the firm. Jacques would have to update the picture again. To my chagrin, I'd been six months pregnant at the time, and the photo wasn't doing me any favors.

Helen frowned at the picture and then pointed at the picture of Zoe. "I didn't know she worked there."

"She's our receptionist. How do you know Zoe?"

Helen pursed her lips. "From church. She never misses a Sunday service." Her eyes narrowed at me and Greg. "Unlike *some* people."

Greg shook his finger at me teasingly.

"Zoe dates that very successful agent," Helen bragged. "Such a charming couple. They're engaged to be married."

"I didn't know Zoe was engaged." She never spoke about her personal life. "What type of an agent is he?"

Helen gave me a funny look. "He's a real estate agent, silly. His name is Jeremy Granger."

My mouth opened in surprise. Jeremy Granger ran one of the most successful agencies in the area. He did twice as much business as Jacques did. I stared at Helen. "Are—are you sure?"

"Of course I'm sure. She introduced me to him herself. He

came to church a couple of weeks ago. I guess he's not Catholic, but the priest will marry them anyway."

"Oh my God." All along I thought it was Stacey who had been giving away the leads, when in fact it was Zoe. How had Jacques and I not realized it was her? She answered the phone more than anyone. She had chosen not to pass on the leads to Jacques and instead was sending them to her prospective husband.

Jacques and Ed were already on their way here, but I stepped into the study to call my boss anyway. He picked up on the first ring.

"Don't get your panties in a bunch. We're almost there."

I sucked out a breath. "It's not that. I think I've solved another mystery, thanks to my mother-in-law."

"Well," Jacques teased. "Maybe we can hire Helen as your new personal assistant. Imagine the fun you two would have working together."

CHAPTER TWENTY-TWO

"You look gorgeous tonight, babe." Greg smiled across the table at me, the blue of his eyes reflecting off the candlesticks between us. "Motherhood definitely agrees with you."

We were at one of the most impressive restaurants in town, The French Delight. I had never been here before, but Greg insisted that we splurge this time—in honor of Valentine's Day, and to celebrate my first big sale. I had ordered ratatouille, and Greg had selected duck in wine sauce. Since I couldn't drink, I was playing designated driver tonight. It was just as well. The last time Greg and I had been out for a fancy dinner was on our 18th wedding anniversary last June. I'd had too much to drink and didn't remember much about that evening. The end result had arrived eight months later, in the form of a beautiful baby girl. Tonight, sparkling water suited me fine.

The lights had been dimmed in the formal dining room, and a pianist was playing a Frank Sinatra song in one corner while a few people sat at the bar talking. Seven or eight other couples were spread throughout the room. At Greg's request, we had been seated in a private booth that looked out on the river. Even though frozen, it was still a lovely view, with the outdoor lights shining on the water's shimmering surface. It made me wish for spring even more.

"As far as looking good, I haven't lost any of the baby weight yet," I reminded him. "I'm up at least twenty pounds."

"Well, I can't tell. You get more beautiful every day." His voice was low and sexy and sent a thrilling chill up my spine. It was wonderful to have some alone time with the love of my life, especially given everything that had happened in the last couple of weeks. Now if I could only figure out how to broach the subject I'd been wanting to speak with him about for a while.

Greg must have noticed my distraction because he raised an eyebrow at me. "Something's bothering you."

"No, I'm fine."

His expression was doubtful. "Please. I know you, remember?"

"Well," I hedged. "During these last few weeks, something has changed for me. I'd forgotten how much I enjoyed spending time with the kids when they were little. I had so much fun with Darcy when I was able to take off work the first year she was born. Then when Stevie and Seth were babies, we were always tired and there wasn't as much time to enjoy them."

He smiled fondly. "How can I forget? Back then, I never knew if I was coming or going. Remember the time I got up and drove to work half asleep before it dawned on me that it was a Sunday?"

I laughed. "That was classic."

He watched me closely, his jaw set in determination. "I think I know what this is about. You don't want to be away from the baby."

It amazed me how in sync we were at times. We could even finish each other's sentences. Sure, this came from being married so long, but it was also the result of caring for and loving someone deeply.

I exhaled a long sigh. "The twins were a lot of work, but I certainly don't love them any less because of it. Grace is our last baby, and I don't want to miss out on that special time again."

"Sweetheart." Greg leaned forward. "Are you trying to say that you want to give up the real estate business and be a full-time stay-at-home mom?"

"I don't know," I confessed. "I love what I do, but this past week it broke my heart every time I had to leave her. Maybe we could try it for a couple of months, or even until the summer, and then Darcy could step in to give me a hand so that I could go back to work on a part-time basis. The commission from Eleanor's house will help for a while too. I realize that staying home for good isn't an option."

A smile creased Greg's face as he reached for his wineglass. "I want whatever will make you happy. But what does Jacques say about it? Or haven't you told him yet?"

"He knows, and he's fine with whatever I decide. He's mentioned my babysitting Bolin when he arrives from China and that he and Ed would insist on paying me."

"That's an interesting name," Greg mused. "Does it have a special meaning?"

"Gentle rain. Isn't that beautiful? I think he'd make a great companion for the twins after school and during vacations. Plus, it will help Jacques and Ed out big-time, too."

Greg leaned back in the chair. "That sounds great. If you want to continue to work or go back at a later date, that's perfectly fine with me. I've got to confess that the idea of you *not* working with cutthroat real estate agents—and I mean it literally—or potential serial killer-like clients has major appeal. I hate having your life in constant danger."

"The twins trying to burn down the house last year doesn't count?" I teased.

He grinned. "Well, you've got me on that one. Those two can be pretty scary some days. Let me say that I would be very happy to not have to worry about someone sticking a gun in my wife's face for a change. I love you and want your happiness more than anything."

I reached my hand across the table. "Thank you for that. For the record, I feel the same way about you."

Greg drew my hand to his lips. "I was hoping you'd say that because I have some news of my own. This may be just the thing to help ensure your happiness."

Now he had my full curiosity. "Oh? Wait—that can only mean one thing. Your mother is moving to Argentina."

Greg roared with such laughter that the people across the room turned to look at us. "Okay, so this might be a close second. I've been offered a promotion. I'll be the new District Manager of the firm. It will mean a bit more traveling, but the raise will ensure that you can stay home—at least until the summer. If you decide to babysit for Jacques and Ed, that will help too. For the record, I haven't accepted the job yet. I told my boss that I needed to speak with you first."

"Oh my God!" I whispered. Greg had been in line for this position at the auto distribution company where he worked for almost ten years. He'd been passed over a few times already, and in my opinion, unfairly. "I'm so proud of you, sweetheart. Yes, I want you to take it. If, like you said, it makes you happy."

His blue eyes were soft as he continued to stare at me. "I've always been happy, but knowing that my beautiful wife is content makes it even better." He raised his glass into the air. "Better days are finally here, my love. For the both of us."

We clinked our glasses together and were silent for a minute as the waiter brought our entrees. Greg picked up his fork and started to eat, offering me a bite. "Want some?"

"It's in wine, so I'd better not. But it looks delicious."

"Tell me something," Greg said. "If your real estate employment is on hold for now, does that mean your sleuthing career is finished as well? You're starting to get quite a reputation in this town."

Boy, didn't I know it. Earlier today a reporter had shown up on our front doorstep, looking to interview me for the local paper. There had also been an article in the day before by a different writer along with a picture of me and a description of a local real estate agent and her "deadly" deals. An author from the area was planning to write a book about Percy's misguided life and had already called to ask for my help. I'd politely declined.

"Who knows?" I shrugged and dug into my ratatouille. "You should never put anything past a Jessica Fletcher wannabe."

ABOUT THE AUTHOR

USA Today bestselling author Catherine lives in Upstate New York with a male dominated household that consists of her very patient husband, three sons, and several spoiled pets. She has wanted to be a writer since the age of eight when she wrote her own version of Cinderella (and fortunately Disney never sued). Catherine has a dual major in both English and Performing Arts. Her book, For Sale by Killer, won the 2019 Daphne du Maurier award for Mainstream Mystery/Suspense. She loves to read, bake and attend live theater performances.

ALSO BY CATHERINE BRUNS

Sign up for Catherine's monthly newsletter and receive a free ebook as a thank you!

Italian Chef Mysteries

Penne Dreadful

It Cannoli be Murder

The Enemy You Gnocchi

Cookies & Chance Mysteries

Tastes Like Murder

Baked to Death

Burned to a Crisp

Frosted with Revenge

Silenced by Sugar

Crumbled to Pieces

Sprinkled in Malice

Ginger Snapped to Death

Icing on the Casket

Knee Deep in Dough

Dessert is the Bomb

Cindy York Mysteries

Killer Transaction

Priced to Kill

For Sale by Killer

Aloha Lagoon Mysteries

Death of the Big Kahuna

Death of the Kona Man

Printed in Great Britain
by Amazon